"There's one thing I don't understand," said Gerber.

"Those VC around the field. You said they were stunned. What happened to them?"

"I shot them." Connel grinned. "They were out of it. They didn't have a clue about what was going on. The strikers didn't shoot much, but we killed them just the same."

Fetterman slammed the table with his hand. "Goddamn great!"

"What are you getting so upset about?" asked Connel. "They were the enemy."

"You don't murder helpless people," said Fetterman.

"That's a damn funny idea from a soldier," countered Connel.

Fetterman lowered his voice. There was a knifelike edge to it. "I'm a soldier, not a murderer."

"But they were VC. If I didn't kill them they'd soon return to kill Americans."

"No," said Gerber. "There are rules against shooting the wounded. They could have been taken prisoner. There was no reason to shoot them. Don't you understand what you've done? Now you've made everything the American press writes about us true. We're supposed to be superior, compassionate, intelligent, but you've made us common killers."

Also available by Eric Helm:

VIETNAM: GROUND ZERO
P.O.W.
UNCONFIRMED KILL
THE FALL OF CAMP A-555
SOLDIER'S MEDAL
THE KIT CARSON SCOUT
THE HOBO WOODS
GUIDELINES
THE VILLE
INCIDENT AT PLEI SOI
TET
THE IRON TRIANGLE
RED DUST
HAMLET
MOON CUSSER
DRAGON'S JAW
CAMBODIAN SANCTUARY
PAYBACK
MACV
TAN SON NHUT
PUPPET SOLDIERS
GUNFIGHTER

THE RAID
SHIFTING FIRES
STRIKE
EMPIRE

VIETNAM: GROUND ZERO™

WARRIOR

ERIC HELM

A GOLD EAGLE BOOK FROM
WORLDWIDE®

TORONTO · NEW YORK · LONDON · PARIS
AMSTERDAM · STOCKHOLM · HAMBURG
ATHENS · MILAN · TOKYO · SYDNEY

First edition April 1990

ISBN 0-373-62723-8

VIETNAM:GROUND ZERO™
WARRIOR

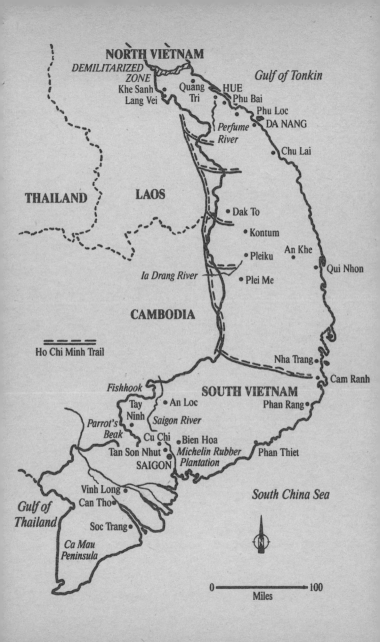

PROLOGUE

For the past hour Marcus Connel had been sitting in the corner booth with a couple of friends, waiting to learn the order in which they would graduate in June. They had been discussing it for more than two weeks and based their estimates on the positions they had held in the cadet battalion, on their grades in the various ROTC courses and finally on their overall academic standing at the university.

Connel was one of the oldest of the group, though he had just turned twenty-two. He sat with his back to the wall so that he could survey everything and everyone in front of him. He was a tall man with blond hair and blue eyes. He had fine features, a square jaw and a Roman nose. His only flaw was his ears. They stuck out just a little more than they should have, and if Army regulations hadn't demanded short hair, he would have worn it long enough to cover them.

He sat with a glass of beer in front of him, lifting it occasionally. He wasn't drinking it fast because he had all afternoon. Everyone there had all afternoon. Finals, for the most part, were finished, and the last of the classes would be held during the next week, but those were little more than a formality. There was nothing to do now except hang around for the graduation ceremonies and then head off to join the American military machine, which was growing daily as the police action in Vietnam drew more heavily on the pool of manpower.

Connel lifted his glass to drain it. Instead he held it high in salute as a long-haired girl entered. She glanced at him, grinned and then came over to sit down.

"Make room for her," said Connel, pointing at Roger MacDonal and Bruce Lawson.

Lawson, a junior in the ROTC, stood up and surrendered his chair. "Here, Sarah. Sit." He then grabbed a chair from a nearby table and pulled it closer.

"Drinking beer?" she asked.

Connel nodded. "There's not much else to do at the moment."

"Drinking beer and winning the war," said MacDonal. He had just turned twenty-one and wasn't used to the privileges of adulthood. He drank too fast, trying to make up for the time he had missed. He was short and stout. His body bordered on fat, and if he hadn't played racquetball twice a week, would have blossomed. He had brown hair that was already beginning to thin.

"Would you care for a beer?" Connel asked her, reaching for the pitcher.

She put her books on the table, no longer caring about keeping them dry. Her notes from four different classes were now worthless. She'd taken her finals.

She was a tall woman, five-eight, and had long blond hair that hung straight down her back. She was skinny, the long hours of studying and the hurrying across the campus keeping her from gaining any weight.

"A beer?" she repeated as if thinking about it. "Yeah. I'd like a beer."

Connel turned over an empty glass, one of a half-dozen spares they had in case someone new entered, filled it from the pitcher and said, "There you go."

She sipped at it and set it down. "What war were you winning?"

"Vietnam," said Connel.

"Uh-huh," she said.

Connel smiled at her, then looked around the bar, which consisted of two rooms, one with a bar and the other with booths in it. Pinball machines stood along one wall, popping, dinging and ringing as students stood around them cheering one another on. There was a table near the front window where students sat watching other students walk by. The air was filled with the mugginess of late spring and the odor of stale beer, vomit and fresh popcorn from the machine at the edge of the bar. A jukebox played in the corner, but it was turned so low that hardly anyone could hear it over the other noise.

"We figure," said MacDonal, "that we're going to be there inside of a year."

"Right," she said sarcastically. "Going off to become war heroes."

"Maybe not heroes," said Connel, "but we're going to end up there." He glanced around the table and then at the young men in the bar. "A lot of us are going to end up there."

"So what are you going to do?" asked Sarah.

Connel looked as if he had an answer, but then didn't speak. Instead Lawson said, "Going to spend my time there trying not to get killed. Survival. That's the key to warfare. You fight so that the enemy dies for his country, and once enough of them have, then the war ends.''

Sarah sipped her beer and tried to keep from smiling. Lawson was so intense. He always had been. Everything was so important and had to be done just right, even if it was a stupid five-page research paper analyzing a ridiculous poem. That didn't matter. He worked on it as if his life were at stake. Or the fate of the free world.

"Not much of a war," she said. "Not much of a threat to the United States."

"But it's the only one we have," said Connel. "So we go kill the enemy."

Sarah looked at him. "That's a pretty bloodthirsty attitude."

"Of course," he said. "But that's what war's all about. You kill the enemy as quickly as you can. You kill them at every opportunity. You give them no quarter."

"Yeah," said MacDonal. "During World War II an American submarine captain put a torpedo into a troop transport and then machine-gunned the Japanese soldiers in the water."

"And you think that's right?" asked Sarah.

"Hell, yes!" said Connel. "If he hadn't done that, those Japanese soldiers might have faced American Marines and killed them within a couple of weeks. You kill the enemy. Period."

Sarah shook her head. "They sure brainwashed you."

"No," said Connel. "They taught us about fighting a war. If you're not prepared to fight it, then you have no business in it. If our government doesn't feel like that, they have no right to order men into combat. You have to be prepared to do what is necessary to win."

"They've turned you into murderers."

"No!" snapped Connel. "They've taught us that you either fight a war or you don't."

"Then you approve of what that man, that submarine man, did during the war?"

"Hell, yes," said Connel. "He was killing enemy soldiers. He was doing his duty."

"They were helpless."

Connel shrugged. "That point is debatable. But the real point is that our Marines didn't end up facing those Japanese soldiers. You win by ending the enemy's will to fight, and you do that by beating them into the ground every chance you get."

Sarah finished her beer. She stared into the faces of the young men she had thought she'd known. Here they were talking easily about killing people. Killing them because they had been labeled as the enemy and for no other reason. That attitude scared her.

"I think I'll be going," she said.

Connel nodded at her, half closing his eyes. "You'll be glad someday there are people who think like we do. Without us around to protect you so that you can hold your ideals, you'd be marching down the street under orders from the government. There would be no one around to stop them. We keep you free so that you can think for yourself."

"I'm not sure that I like that," she said.

"I'm not sure that it matters all that much," said Connel. "As long as we're around to protect you."

She picked up her books, glanced at each of the young men and then walked for the door.

"Well," said Lawson.

"Gentlemen," said Connel. "Civilians don't know shit, and that's why they're civilians."

1

NEAR THE HO CHI MINH TRAIL JUST INSIDE CAMBODIA JUNE 1968

Although the sun was at its zenith, it was still dim inside the triple-canopy jungle. A haze, one born of humidity, of heat, of monsoon rains that never reached the ground but filtered through the trees, drifted on a light breeze. The haze was white like woodsmoke, which made it seem as if the jungle had caught fire.

Army Special Forces Captain MacKenzie K. Gerber crouched at the base of one of the teak trees, a knee resting in the rotting vegetation. In his left hand he held an M-16, the butt resting against his thigh. His attention was focused on the Ho Chi Minh Trail, barely visible through the thick vegetation in front of him.

Gerber was a young man by societal standards, but old for a combat officer. At thirty he was still prowling the jungle while most officers his age and with his experience had found their way into staff jobs that were good for career development. Gerber refused to do that, preferring to stay in the field where he could accomplish something important.

After many months in Vietnam, Gerber was lean, almost gaunt. His brown hair had grown out so that it was longer than regulations allowed, but the men in the field sometimes let such things slide. Gerber was tall, had blue eyes and was deceptively strong.

There was a rustling to his right and Gerber glanced in that direction. Hidden among the patches of dark and light, the deep greens and the deeper browns, he saw the face of Master Sergeant Anthony B. Fetterman. Fetterman was a small, balding man whose hair had begun its retreat as he'd advanced across Omaha Beach during the Normandy Invasion. He was dark with a heavy beard that required two shaves a day or it looked as if he hadn't in three or four.

Now he moved from his cover, slipping to the right and making very little noise. Gerber knew the master sergeant could slide through the jungle like a morning fog, disturbing nothing, so that the noise he made now was to alert Gerber that he was coming closer.

"Traffic has stopped," he said, his lips no more than six inches from Gerber's ear.

"What's that make it?"

"In three days we've seen fourteen bicycles and twenty-seven soldiers armed with AKs. Not very much."

Gerber nodded and understood exactly what Fetterman was telling him. The enemy, the Vietcong, had been destroyed during the Tet offensive. A hundred thousand VC soldiers had attacked cities and military targets all over South Vietnam, and when the smoke had cleared, better than two-thirds had been killed, wounded or captured.

After the Tet disaster, the North Vietnamese had begun to filter into the South in greater numbers, but the rumored attack against Saigon didn't come. Instead the flow of supplies, men and equipment along the infiltration routes, including the Ho Chi Minh Trail, had slowed to a trickle.

"Maybe they're heading into Two Corps for the Central Highlands," Gerber suggested.

"I don't know, sir. I'd think they'd want to get someone into Three Corps."

"You happy with the observations here, Tony?"

Fetterman nodded slowly. "Yes, sir."

"Then you're ready to pull out?"

Fetterman glanced at his watch and then up into the canopy. There was no way for him to tell where the sun was. Light filtered through, but it turned the ground into a glowing green hell with minimal visibility. There were flashes of color from the flowers on bushes and the plumage of birds that sometimes dived out of the trees. The canopy above them was alive with monkeys, lizards and rodents.

Looking back at Gerber, Fetterman said, "If we hurry, we can get back into South Vietnam by dark."

"But not early enough for pickup. Choppers won't land that close to the border this close to nightfall."

"Be safer for us in South Vietnam," said Fetterman.

Gerber wasn't sure the master sergeant was right. Operations inside Cambodia were illegal and everyone knew it. Charlie and the North Vietnamese didn't pay as much attention to military techniques there as they did on the other side of the border.

Of course, once they were inside South Vietnam they could call on artillery and fighters if they got into trouble. There were reinforcements if they were needed. It was a toss-up, and Gerber didn't know the real answer.

"If you're satisfied with what we've seen," said Gerber, "let's get out of here."

"Yes, sir. Twenty minutes."

Gerber nodded and turned his attention back to the Ho Chi Minh Trail. He could see a small section of it, no more than six or seven feet, but even with that he could tell that *trail* was the wrong word. It was a road, a highway that led from North Vietnam into the South. Portions of it were paved with pea gravel, giving it a surface as hard and durable as some of the superhighways built back in the World. Bridges along the Trail, Gerber knew, were built a foot or so underwater. That way, if an Air Force pilot managed to see all the way to the ground, he wouldn't be able to spot the bridge.

Slowly he stood up, keeping his right shoulder against the smooth bark of the teak tree. He glanced to the left and saw three of the Vietnamese strikers who had accompanied them on the patrol. Two were dressed in sweat-soaked fatigues and the third in black pajamas. Each held an M-16.

They slipped away from the line, disappearing into the jungle. Gerber followed them and then saw Fetterman off to the right. The rest of the patrol, another dozen Vietnamese strikers, joined the first group. Like them, they were dressed in jungle fatigues or black pajamas.

When they were assembled there, Fetterman lifted his hand and pointed back to the east. Then he turned and began working his way into the jungle. He vanished in a moment, lost in the dimness of the jungle and the shifting patterns of green, brown and black that disguised everything and everyone.

The men strung out behind him, separated by two or three yards so that each man could see the one in front of him but not the head of the patrol. Such a precaution improved the odds that an ambush set anywhere along the path would probably not get everyone and that a booby trap would take out the man who tripped it but no one else.

Gerber brought up the rear. He glanced back and then moved along with the others, dodging low-hanging branches and stepping over fallen trees and around bushes. The captain moved slowly, placing his feet carefully. He felt the ground in front of him with his toe, probing for a twig that would snap or a trip wire that would detonate a booby trap. Searching the jungle around him, he looked for things that didn't belong—a motion that was unnatural, a color that didn't fit in with the rest of the background.

They moved for ten minutes and then halted, slipping to the right and left, forming a rough circle. Gerber faced the rear, watching their trail. After only a few minutes, they were moving again, sliding through the jungle, trying to leave no sign for an enemy to follow.

Fetterman halted them after seven minutes, rested for two and then was moving again. He stopped after another twelve minutes, rested for five and was off again. By varying the time and distance traveled, he hoped to cause anyone who might be shadowing them to make a mistake and reveal themselves.

They kept moving through the heat of the afternoon. Humidity hung in the air. Sweat soaked their uniforms and it became difficult to move as the heat sapped their strength.

After three hours they finally stopped. In the distance they could hear the rumble of artillery, while overhead, invisible through the triple-canopy jungle, jets thundered by. Gerber slipped forward, moving among the strikers until he found Fetterman crouched behind a massive log.

"I think we're back in South Vietnam," said Fetterman. He pointed to the one-o'clock position. "And we've got someone over there."

Gerber turned and stared into the thick jungle but couldn't see anything. The undergrowth was too thick, and everything was locked in shadow.

Vines, bushes, saplings and ferns were in the way. Water dripping through the canopy coupled with the cries of windmilling birds and the chatter of monkeys to make it difficult to hear any enemy movement.

Gerber leaned close to the master sergeant, ignoring the odor that was the result of a long patrol in the jungle. "Don't see anything."

"Ten guys," said Fetterman.

Gerber nodded. "Ours or theirs?"

"That I don't know. Hold the men here and I'll go take a look."

"Fifteen minutes."

"Shouldn't need more than that." He moved forward, crouched and finally slipped off into the jungle.

Gerber stayed there for a moment, listening, but Fetterman was as quiet as the afternoon breeze. He made no sound at all. Gerber settled down, one knee on the thick cushion of fallen leaves, bits of bark and the rotting remains of trees. He kept his eyes moving and his ears open, but the only thing he saw was the jungle, and the only sounds he heard were made by animals.

Fetterman reappeared suddenly a few minutes later, as if he had sprouted instantaneously from the jungle floor. He leaned in close and whispered, "Eleven men. Two in NVA khaki and the others dressed as Vietcong.

They're all armed with AKs. Couple of grenades visible but no pistols.''

"An ambush?"

"No, sir. Campsite, I think. Afternoon rest and then they'll be moving with the last of the sun."

"Let's take them," said Gerber.

Fetterman grinned. "I was hoping you'd say that."

"Quietly, one by one. I'd like to get some prisoners out of this. Maybe they can tell us what in hell's going on out here."

"Yes, sir."

"Okay, let's get the men ready. I want two to stay back here with the extra equipment. We use knives until there's a shot, and then we use the rifles."

"Yes, sir."

"Let's do it."

Together they worked their way back through the jungle and collected their soldiers. The Vietnamese strikers formed a loose circle around Gerber and Fetterman.

Pointing to two men, Gerber said, "You'll remain here, guarding the gear."

One man nodded and the other said, "Yes, Dai Uy."

"Tony."

Fetterman used his index finger to draw the enemy encampment in the dirt. "We've got eleven guys. Guards are here and here. The rest are scattered in here in a circle, facing out. We'll have to take them all at once after we've taken out the guards." Fetterman glanced at Gerber. "Sir. I'll take the guard here. You want the other one?"

"I'll take him."

"Once that's done," continued Fetterman, "we infiltrate and take the rest of them. Knives first, but as soon as there's a shot use the rifles. Questions?"

"Prisoners," said Gerber.

Fetterman nodded. "Let's take a prisoner or two. A dead man can tell us some things, but a prisoner can tell us a lot more." He fell silent.

Gerber touched his combat knife. It was in a scabbard taped upside down to his harness, which made drawing it easier. He nodded at the men.

"We ready," said the Vietnamese NCO.

"Tony."

Fetterman turned. He shrugged his way out of his rucksack, dropping it onto the ground. Then he made sure he still had his first aid kit, two hand grenades and a bandolier of ammo for his M-16.

Gerber followed suit, dropping his gear onto the ground near Fetterman's. He then moved forward and was swallowed up by the jungle.

The Vietnamese did the same and then fanned out behind Gerber and Fetterman. The master sergeant waited until he saw that everyone was ready, then moved forward slowly. He ducked under a low-hanging branch and crouched, his fingers brushing the jungle floor.

They all moved quietly, following Fetterman. They eased their way deeper into the jungle. Fetterman finally held up a hand and stopped them. He pointed to the right toward a huge tree with roots that stuck up through the ground like the fingers of a giant hand.

Gerber caught movement among the vines and saplings that seemed to be clinging to the trunk of the huge tree. Staring into the shadows and between the long, flat leaves of a vine, he saw the head and shoulders of an enemy soldier. The man was smoking a cigarette. Its orange tip was visible against the dark background of the jungle shadows, and the motion of the man's hand drew attention to him.

Fetterman pointed to the left, and Gerber knew that was where the second guard was hidden. He nodded and pointed to the right, telling Fetterman he would take that man.

They separated. Gerber slipped to his right, moving so that the guard wouldn't be able to see him. The bulk of the tree would hide him from the Vietcong. He stayed low, moving slowly, cautiously. He was bent nearly double, the fingers of his left hand touching the ground as if he were feeling his way along it. He glanced at the man, not wanting to stare at him. Concentrating on the target sometimes alerted it.

He reached the side of the tree and lost sight of the enemy. Before he moved in he checked the jungle around him. There was no sign of any other enemy soldiers. Gerber then stepped forward and leaned against the tree. He could smell the smoke from the cigarette.

Slowly he turned, crouched and slipped to the right, looking up. He caught a glimpse of the Vietcong, and as the man looked away, Gerber attacked. He came up suddenly, stepping in close. Clamping a hand over the enemy's nose and mouth, he pushed the soldier back, forcing him into the tree. As the man fell to the rear against the trunk, Gerber struck with his knife. The razor-sharp blade cut through the rough cloth of the uniform and punctured the skin. Forcing the knife upward under the ribs, he pierced the man's lung and heart. Blood pumped from the wound, splashing down and covering Gerber's hand. The odor of fresh copper filled the air, overpowering the cigarette smoke.

The man groaned once, low in the throat, and sagged. Carefully Gerber lowered the body to the ground. He looked into the dead man's staring, unseeing eyes. They had yet to glaze over. They still looked alive and terrified.

Gerber crouched and pulled the AK from the dead man's hands. He set it against the tree, then put a hand on the VC's throat to make sure there was no pulse. Satisfied, he moved back around to the side, where he stood looking into the trees. A moment later Fetterman appeared and held a thumb up.

Gerber watched as the rest of the men began to move again. They worked their way forward. Gerber held where he was but unslung his rifle. He came around the tree and halted for a moment.

One of his men slipped toward the enemy soldiers. He came up behind the VC, grabbed him around the face and jerked him to the rear. The knife flashed and blood spurted. The striker lowered the dead man to the ground.

Then there was a sudden burst of gunfire—an AK on full-auto. Bullets snapped through the air, hitting tree trunks. Gerber dropped to one knee, aimed, but found no target. He didn't move.

There was more firing—single shots and then a burst from an M-16, followed by a scream of pain and a crash as someone fell into the jungle.

"Grenade!" yelled Fetterman.

Gerber waited, then heard a single, distant explosion. Dirt and debris fountained upward and rained back. The odor of cordite filled the air as well as the shouts of his Vietnamese strikers.

A man burst from cover. He held an AK and wore a khaki-colored pith helmet. Gerber tracked him and aimed. He pulled the trigger, missed and fired again. The round hit the enemy soldier in the back, lifted him and threw him onto the ground.

"Coming at you, Captain," yelled Fetterman.

Gerber turned. Someone was running through the jungle. He could hear him. He whirled, crouched and waited. The man burst from cover, and as he did, Gerber stood up. He swung his M-16 and knocked the man down. The enemy flipped over and tried to roll away, but Gerber stooped and pointed the barrel of his rifle at the man's face.

The enemy soldier stopped moving. He stared at the rifle, his eyes widening. The man was frozen with fear.

There was another burst, this time from an M-16. Then Fetterman yelled, "That's got it, Captain!"

Gerber motioned to the man on the ground. "Get up," he ordered.

The soldier complied, moving slowly, his eyes fixed on Gerber as he got to his feet. He raised his hands over his head and faced the captain.

"Turn around," Gerber barked.

They moved into the campsite. Seven bodies lay there, their equipment scattered all around. One rifle had been broken in half and another was stuck in the ground. A cooking pot lay on its side and a fire that had been built to cook rice was beginning to smoke. There were a couple of rucksacks lying on the ground, along with a radio and four chest pouches holding spare AK-47 magazines. Two men stood with their hands over their heads.

"Rest of them are dead, Captain."

"What about the people on our side?"

"One dead, one wounded. Wound's not bad, though."

Gerber checked his watch. "If we get to the LZ, we might be able to get a chopper now that we've got a wounded man."

"Map showed an LZ about half a klick from here. Not very large, though."

"We don't need a big one," said Gerber. "Two ships will cover us."

Fetterman glanced at the prisoners, who were all standing together with their hands locked behind their necks, looking as if they expected to get shot at any moment. They kept their eyes on the ground, hoping that if they didn't make eye contact they would be allowed to live a little longer.

"Tony," said Gerber, "get on the radio and see what you can do about getting us some aviation support. Should be someone around who can help us."

"Yes, sir. And then?"

"We'll take the wounded to the hospital and get the prisoners into Saigon so that they can be interrogated by Military Intelligence."

"You think they'll be able to tell us anything?"

Gerber shrugged. "Who knows?"

2

TAN SON NHUT SAIGON

Second Lieutenant Marcus Connel waited impatiently for the stewardess to unlock the front hatch so that he, along with all the other new guys, could escape into Vietnam. He had been warned, as they all had, that the plane would be on the ground for only a few minutes and that they were to exit rapidly. Charlie sometimes tried to blow up commercial jets with mortars and rockets, and the plane's captain didn't want to sit there any longer than he had to.

Finally, with the aisle filled with waiting soldiers, the hatch was opened and they surged forward. As an officer, Connel was near the front of the plane. He ducked down, stepped through the hatch and found himself on a ramp that led to the tarmac below him.

He took his first breath of Vietnamese air. It was hot, humid and tasted of burnt kerosene and burnt gunpowder. He felt sweat bead immediately as he began to descend to the ground. To the west were thunderheads, but the sun was still bright over him. The reflected tropical light made him blink rapidly and squint.

As he reached the ground, an MP wearing sweat-soaked, shapeless jungle fatigues and holding a fully loaded M-16 said, "On the bus, sir."

Connel stopped and glanced at it. It was an old Army vehicle painted a sickly OD green with dents along the side, mud splattered around the wheels and what looked like a bullet hole in the door. There were heavy screens over the windows and a metal sheet over half the windshield.

None of that made an impression on Connel. He didn't care about the bus or the hangars behind it. Instead he was excited about being in Vietnam. He, like a long line of men before him, was now in a war zone. He was one of the long, green line of men who had marched off to war. With him now in Vietnam, could victory be far behind? No one, nothing, could stop an American soldier when he set his mind to achieving a goal.

He turned and watched the men stream from the aircraft, down to the tarmac and right up into the bus. They wore a variety of uniforms—Army khakis, fatigues, Air Force blues. Two hundred men all told who had joined the war effort.

"Finally," he said.

He climbed into the bus and worked his way toward the back. The interior was dim and hot and smelled of diesel fumes. But Connel didn't care. This was the vehicle that was going to take him into battle.

When the bus was filled, the guard stepped up into it and the driver shut the door. They rumbled to the right, then drove between two hangars and off the airfield.

Connel turned and studied Tan Son Nhut. There were jet fighters in sandbagged revetments. Men with yellow equipment worked on some of them. Armed guards patrolled the perimeters of the airfield. There were low buildings, a story or two high, with corrugated tin roofs and sandbags that were stacked four or five feet high around the walls.

They turned a corner and followed a narrow road. Neatly trimmed grass grew around two-story buildings painted white. There were trees and bushes near the building but very little ground clutter, an obvious attempt to keep cover away from attacking soldiers if the enemy managed to penetrate the perimeter.

He tried to see everything, ducking down so that he could look out the window opposite him. The flight line stretched out in front of him, looking like an international airport except that there were revetments for jet fighters guarded by armed soldiers.

They turned again and the airfield vanished. Beyond the chain-link fence topped with barbed wire were the streets of Saigon. Hundreds of Vietnamese pedestrians moved along the fence. Many of the men were dressed in light pants and shirts. Some of the women wore short skirts, while others were dressed in traditional garb. GIs circulated among the civilians.

That scene disappeared behind a building and then the bus stopped. As the door opened, the guard stepped down. Connel wondered if the man was for show. They hadn't driven off the base and no one had even yelled at them. No one seemed to care that they had arrived in Vietnam.

A fat sergeant wearing faded jungle fatigues and gray boots stepped from a small doorway in the side of a hangar and yelled, ''In here.''

Connel waited while the rest of the men filed off the bus and through the door, then he followed them and found a large room that was open at one end. Fans stood on the polished concrete floor, trying to cool things off but doing nothing more than blowing around the hot air and making a great deal of noise.

There were several rows of folding chairs where the men who had been on the bus now sat. The fat sergeant stood in front of them, his hands on his hips, watching. He was standing so that one of the fans was blowing right on his back. He was the only man who looked comfortable.

When everyone had found a seat, the sergeant moved away from the fan. Raising his voice, he yelled, "I ain't gonna welcome ya to Vietnam 'cause I know none of ya is happy to be here. Point is, ya're here and ya got a year to stay, and if ya don't fuck up, ya'll go home."

"Jesus," said Connel under his breath.

"Tamarra, ya'll have to be back here so that we can get ya out to the field. Those of ya goin' to infantry companies might get a week here for a general orientation school. The rest of ya will get orders and ya can head up-country or down-country."

He wiped a hand over his sweat-damp face. "Ya'll all get quarters tonight in Saigon, here on the base." He pointed to a small table to the right, where a rock held down a stack of paper. "There's a list of things that ya'll need to know. Grab one and be back here at eight."

"Quarter assignments?" asked one of the sergeants who had just arrived.

"Yeah," the fat NCO said, nodding. "Climb on the bus and it'll take ya to the transient quarters. Officers first, then NCOs and finally the enlisted pukes. Questions?"

"We free until tomorrow?" asked someone.

"Yeah. Ya can go downtown and pick up a dose or get drunk or whatever. Leave most of your money here and watch out for the whores. Be here tamarra at eight."

Connel sat there surprised. He'd expected someone telling him about the war. He'd expected some advice on how to pass the year, and he'd expected a few words about what might happen to him in the next few days. Instead he got a fat, bored sergeant telling them not to bother him until eight the next morning.

The men began to file out of the room and toward the bus. Again Connel let them all get out before he followed them. Rather than sit down in the back of the bus, he stood near the guard at the front and waited.

They drove away from the small hangar and stopped a moment later near a single-story building. Sandbags were stacked on either side of the door and there were open windows along the sides.

"Officers' quarters," said the driver as he leaned over to open the door.

Connel got off the bus and found a pile of luggage sitting on the sidewalk. He found his duffel bag, then walked toward the door and opened it. Inside was a small room with a waist-high counter, behind which sat a man in a sweat-soaked OD T-shirt.

"Have you got a room for Lieutenant Connel?" he asked the clerk.

"I don't have a room for a Lieutenant Connel, but I do have some vacant rooms. I'll need a copy of your travel orders."

Connel dropped his bag onto the floor near the door and walked over to the counter. He set his briefcase down, opened it and pulled out a copy of his orders, which he handed to the clerk.

"Oh, an FNG. Welcome to Vietnam, Lieutenant."

"Thanks."

"How long you going to be here?"

Connel shrugged. "Tonight at least. The sergeant on the welcoming committee suggested there was some kind of orientation period before I get orders."

"Check in again tomorrow and let me know," he said. He pushed a card across the desk. "Fill this out."

"Yeah."

Connel filled out the card and was given a key with a plastic tag on it. He picked up his duffel bag and walked down the narrow hallway. Dirty, unpainted plywood covered the floor, and the plywood walls were painted light green. From the interiors of some of the rooms he could hear radios playing loudly, while fans roared in other rooms.

Connel found his room, unlocked the door and shoved it open. There was a military cot pushed against one wall, a dresser that had seen better days against another wall, a chair in the corner and a bamboo mat on the filthy floor. Opposite him there was an open window, but the room was still stifling.

Dropping his duffel bag in the corner near the chair, he walked to the window to see if he could open it farther, but it was wide open. There was no air conditioner, no fan, nothing to cool the room.

And there was no radio or TV, though he did have a copy of the latest *Stars and Stripes* on the dresser. That was the extent of his entertainment opportunities.

"Fuck it," muttered Connel. He turned, left the room and walked back down the hall. He started to leave the barracks, then stopped, turned around and walked back to the counter. "How do I get downtown?"

"First thing you want to do is climb into some civilian clothes. Then just step outside and grab a cab. Vietnamese run them all night long."

"We let them on base, even late at night?"

The man laughed. "Hell, sir, the Vietcong have yet to launch an attack from the back of a cab."

"Seems like a pretty slack way to run things."

"People need the cabs," said the man.

Connel returned to his room, changed into wrinkled civilian clothes, then headed back outside. He stood at the end of the sidewalk for a couple of minutes. A battered cab slipped out of the traffic and stopped close to him. Connel tried to guess the color of the vehicle, but the paint was so faded that it looked like rusted metal with no paint at all.

"Where you go, GI?"

Connel rubbed his chin. He had no idea where he wanted to go. He looked at the driver—a small Vietnamese man in rumpled, dirty clothes. Connel opened the rear door and started to get in but stopped. The back seat was covered with grime. Beer cans littered the floor, along with crumpled newspapers, half a sandwich and a filthy sock. Taking a deep breath, he climbed into the back and slammed the door. Sitting on the edge of the seat, he leaned forward and said, "I want to go downtown."

"Tu Do Street?"

That was a name Connel recognized. Instructors at Benning had talked about Tu Do Street. It was where everyone went when they got in from the field.

"Yeah. Tu Do Street."

The driver dropped the cab into gear, and without bothering to look, pulled out into traffic. There was a squeal of brakes, but the driver didn't seem to notice.

At the front gate Connel saw a small sandbagged structure in the center of the road. It looked like a bunker and was armed with an M-60 machine gun and two guards with M-16s.

They slowed and were waved through. On the other side there was a line of vehicles waiting to enter, and on the sidewalk where a single MP stood at a pedestrian gate, there was a long line of Vietnamese men and women who worked on the base. They were waiting to be cleared by the guard.

Eventually the cab found itself immersed in traffic again—small scooters with one or two people, Lambrettas that held five or six passengers, cars, trucks and military vehicles, some of them bristling with machine guns. On the sidewalks there were hundreds of soldiers in jungle fatigues and khaki. And there were women. Lots of women. For some reason Connel hadn't expected to see women. He'd thought that his year in Vietnam would be without female contact. There weren't any American women, but there were a lot of Vietnamese, all of them dressed in short skirts and light blouses. Many of them were hanging on to Americans.

The taxi turned another corner. Now there were bars and clubs lining the sidewalk. Rock and roll and country and western music blared from the interiors. Near the doors of some of the bars were groups of men drinking beer they had bought inside and others who were waiting for a chance to push their way in.

"Anywhere along here," said Connel.

The driver darted out of the traffic and slammed on the brakes, sliding to a halt. Grinning, he turned and said, "You pay me one thousand P."

Connel wasn't familiar with the term. Instead he said, "I'll give you two dollars."

"One thousand P."

"No way, man," said Connel. He stared at the Vietnamese driver and realized he hated the man. The guy spoke broken English, was a terrible driver and had no sense of cleanliness. The garbage rotting in the back of the cab proved that.

"Hey, Joe. You give me eight hundred P."

"Three bucks," said Connel. "And that's it." He opened the door and climbed out of the cab. Then ducked and looked in the passenger window. The driver was gripping the wheel, his knuckles turning white. Connel waved the three dollars at him. "Three bucks."

"Four bucks," said the driver.

Connel was tiring of the game. He pulled a fourth bill from his wallet and tossed the cash into the front of the cab. "Four bucks, you crook." He whirled and walked away.

As the cab rocketed back into the flow of traffic, Connel stopped. He watched it dodge between two military trucks, looking as if it were about to be crushed, then it vanished.

With the cab gone, Connel surveyed the street. All around him people were talking, a babble of conversation that was nearly buried by the roar of traffic on the street and the rock and roll boiling out of the bars. Sweat-drenched GIs holding cans of beer stood talking to one another or to short Vietnamese women who were no taller than junior high students back in the World.

Connel pushed his way through the crowd and reached the door of the bar. Outside it was hot and humid, but inside was worse. The heat was stifling. He forced himself through the doorway and stood there as his ears were assaulted by the driving beat of the music. Men yelled at one another or shouted encouragement to a woman dancing in a small cage suspended four or five feet above the floor.

Connel moved toward the bar. Before he reached it, a woman grabbed his hand and pulled him toward her.

She leaned close and rubbed herself against him. "Hey, GI, you buy me Saigon Tea?"

"No."

"Hey. You cheap Charlie."

Connel pulled his arm free. "Why don't you just get the hell away from me?"

She stared at him for a moment, then let go of his arm. As she slipped into the crowd, she yelled, "You numbah ten GI!"

Connel reached the bar and leaned forward. There were two Vietnamese men working behind it. Both looked as if they had just stepped from showers. The rowdy GIs were keeping them busy. Connel took out a dollar and waved it at one of the men. The bartender saw the greenback and stopped. "You want?"

"Beer. Bring me a beer."

The man dived into a cooler and surfaced with a Budweiser. "Beer," he said, holding the can up.

Connel took it and surrendered his dollar. He took a drink of the beer and turned to watch the dancer in the cage. She wore only a bikini and knee-high boots. Her body glistened with sweat as she strained to stay with the driving rock and roll beat. Her black hair flew as she pumped her arms.

Then music stopped a moment later and the girl slowed down. She stood there for a moment, her hands on her hips as she tried to catch her breath. Then she straightened, reached down into her bikini bottoms, pulled out some cotton balls and tossed them into the crowd.

"Good Christ," said Connel, disgusted. He tipped back his beer and drank deeply.

He'd been in Vietnam for only a few hours and already he was beginning to hate the Vietnamese. They were a disgusting, worthless people who couldn't be counted on to do a thing for themselves. Their women were filthy, their soldiers cowardly and their politicians corrupt. Now he was in Vietnam to risk his life so that all these people, whose only motivation seemed to be acquiring money, could continue to do that. Thousands of Americans, hundreds of thousands, were there so that the South Vietnamese government could continue to exist.

"For what?" asked Connel, but no one around him bothered to answer. They were too busy watching the woman, hoping she would take off the little she wore and waving money at her as an enticement.

Connel drained his beer and slammed the can onto the bar. He wiped the sweat from his face and rubbed it on his shirt, then started to leave, but another woman grabbed at him. "Hey, you. GI."

"Fuck off!" yelled Connel, pushing her. "Just get the fuck away from me!" She stumbled away and disappeared into the crowd.

Connel reached the door and shoved his way out into the cooler night. He glanced to the right at the entrance to an alley. In a shadow he saw a soldier, his pants around his ankles. A woman had her bare legs wrapped around his waist. She clung to him with her arms and bounced up and down on him in full view of the street.

"Christ," said Connel. "Welcome to fucking Vietnam." He was unaware of the irony of his words.

3

JUNGLES JUST EAST OF
THE CAMBODIAN
BORDER THREE CORPS

The sun had slipped from the sky and it was getting dark in the jungle. Fetterman, with half the Vietnamese, had circled the small LZ, making sure Charlie wasn't hiding nearby. They had moved slowly, at times nearly crawling through the dense vegetation, but they found no sign that Charlie had been there recently. Abandoned bunkers, most of them looking as if they'd been destroyed by American engineers, were scattered around the perimeter. Fetterman found the remains of a rifle, and one of the Vietnamese found a broken combat knife.

Returning to the starting point, Fetterman told Gerber, "Area's secure."

"All right. I want two people guarding our trail and two each at the ends of the LZ. And two more of them to watch our prisoners."

"Do you want anyone on the other side of the LZ?" asked Fetterman.

Gerber shook his head. "We get gun support and that'll be a place for them to suppress." He grinned. "Give them a reason to fire their weapons."

"Yes, sir."

Gerber moved to the RTO and took the handset of the radio, pressing it against his right ear. "Band-Aid Control, this is Zulu Six."

"Go, Six."

"Ah, roger, we've reached an LZ and are requesting pickup. One wounded and one dead. Thirteen alive." He didn't mention the prisoners.

"Roger, Six. Wait one."

Gerber crouched on the ground and wiped the sweat from his forehead. He'd hoped that once the sun was gone the heat would break, but that hadn't happened. Even without the sun it was hot, humid and miserable. The only good thing was that Band-Aid, an Army Aviation unit, was thinking about picking them up. That would save them a two-day walk.

"Zulu Six, this is Band-Aid Operations. We have two aircraft inbound your location. Say condition of LZ."

"Lima Zulu is cold. Negative contact with enemy forces for six hours."

"Roger, that."

Gerber handed the handset back to the RTO, then moved through the jungle until he found Fetterman. The master sergeant was sitting with his back against a tree, eating crackers from a can.

"Be about ten minutes," said Gerber.

Fetterman nodded and stood up. He brushed the dirt from the seat of his uniform and swallowed the last of his crackers. "I'll do a quick swing to make sure Charlie hasn't tumbled to us."

"Then get the men ready to form up. Two loads. Wounded and dead on one ship. Prisoners on the other."

"Yes, sir."

One of the Vietnamese loomed out of the darkness. He stared at Gerber and Fetterman before crouching in front of them. "Someone come."

"Tony?"

"I'm on it, sir." Fetterman dropped the empty can onto the ground and crushed it with his foot. He wiped the crumbs from his mouth and shifted the rifle to his right hand.

"I've got the choppers inbound."

"Roger that, sir."

Gerber turned and walked back to the RTO. He grabbed the handset and said, "Band-Aid OPs, this is Zulu Six."

"Go, six."

"Say ETA."

"Ah, roger, contact Band-Aid One-Five."

"Roger. Break, break. Band-Aid One-Five, this is Zulu Six."

"Roger, Six."

"Say ETA."

"We are zero-five from your reported location. Can you throw smoke, or do you have a strobe?"

"Roger to both."

Again Gerber gave the handset back to the RTO. He moved deeper into the jungle, crouched and listened. Over the usual jungle noises he could hear the muffled sounds of human footsteps.

Then Fetterman appeared. "Don't know who they are. They're a good ten, twelve minutes from us."

"If the choppers hurry, we'll be gone before they can reach us."

"Exactly."

Gerber returned to the RTO and used the handset. "Band-Aid One-Five, this is Zulu Six."

"Go."

"We have unidentified troops approaching from the west. Estimate arrival in one-two minutes."

"Roger. Can you throw smoke now?"

Gerber looked at the RTO. "Throw some yellow smoke into the LZ."

The man moved to the edge of the clearing, looking out into it, then tossed the grenade. In the rapidly fading light the smoke was little more than a dim cloud drifting eastward.

"Smoke out," said Gerber.

"Nothing, Six," said Band-Aid One-Five.

Fetterman appeared at his side. "Those guys are pushing closer, Captain."

Gerber could now hear the faint beat of the rotors. He glanced to the north. In the charcoal sky stars were just beginning to show. The helicopters had to be out there, but he couldn't see them. "Tony, use a strobe."

Fetterman nodded and pulled the pen-sized light from his pocket. He turned it on and pointed it at the sound of the choppers.

"We have a strobe, Zulu Six," Band-Aid One-Five told Gerber.

"Roger." Gerber gave the handset back to the RTO, then found Fetterman. "Let's get the men out into the LZ."

Fetterman handed him the strobe and took off, disappearing in seconds. The Vietnamese began to straggle out of the jungle a moment later. Two men, carrying the body of the dead man wrapped tightly in a poncho liner, worked their way toward the front of the LZ. They set the body on the ground, then crouched in the knee-high grass, almost vanishing from sight. Those with the prisoners started the second load.

The rest of the men filtered out and divided themselves into two loads for the helicopters. They formed small circles to one side of the LZ, each man covering his partner.

"We have the LZ in sight," said Band-Aid One-Five. "We'll touch down in about six-zero seconds."

"Roger," said the RTO.

Fetterman came back. "Everyone's accounted for."

"Then let's get out there."

Gerber and Fetterman, along with the RTO, joined the second load. Now the helicopters were easily visible. The roar of the turbines and the pop of the blades drew attention to them, while their navigation lights flashed dimly.

As they reached the loads, the helicopters crossed over into the LZ. A landing light stabbed out, illuminated the men on the ground, then winked out.

"Shit," said Fetterman. "Nothing like spotlighting us for the enemy.

The aircraft flared, forcing the rotor wash forward. It hit them like the beginning of a hurricane. Loose grass, dirt, leaves and the remnants of the smoke were caught in the whirlwind, causing Gerber to lose sight of the trees around him.

And then suddenly the aircraft was on the ground near him. Two of the Vietnamese strikers stood up and scrambled into the cargo compartment. Gerber waited as the others herded the prisoners, spreading out in the rear of the chopper. He glanced northward and saw that the other men had already gotten into the chopper.

As he stepped up onto the skid, there was a sudden chattering behind him, a faint sound that barely penetrated the roar of the engine and the pop of the blades. Gerber recognized it immediately—an RPD. He dived forward, sprawling on the rough metal of the cargo compartment deck. The M-60 in the gunner's well opened fire then, the ammo rattling out of the can and up into the weapon. A three-foot-long muzzle-flash lanced away from the chopper.

Just as Gerber dived into the chopper, it lifted off, hanging in midair for an instant as the pilot made sure everyone was out of the LZ. Then the nose dropped and the aircraft raced toward the far end of the clearing.

Gerber twisted around to look out. The jungle was alive with enemy soldiers. The ground around the bases of the trees twinkled as if populated with fireflies. But Gerber knew better. The flashing was caused by a dozen or more enemy weapons. Bullets snapped through the air, some of them slamming through the light metal of the tail boom, while tracers crisscrossed the LZ.

The prisoners were sprawled on the deck behind the pilots' seats. They tried to get as close to the armored seats as possible, hoping for some protection there. The striker guarding them watched carefully, ignoring the shooting outside the chopper.

An instant later the LZ was gone and the enemy out of sight. The chopper stayed close to the black jungle. The hammering of the door gun had stopped and the pilot was now beginning to climb out.

"Close!" yelled Fetterman.

"Yeah," agreed Gerber. He sat up and glanced at the Vietnamese strikers in the aircraft. They were sitting on the deck calmly or were climbing up onto the troop seat. Each held his weapon in both hands, the barrel pointed up as they had been taught to do. The prisoners hadn't moved. "Anyone hit?"

One by one the men shook their heads. Satisfied with that, Gerber moved forward so that he was positioned between the two pilots. He tapped the copilot on the shoulder.

The man turned around and stared at him. "What?"

Gerber hooked a thumb over his shoulder and yelled, "What about the enemy?"

"Back there?"

"Yeah."

"We've alerted our operations. They're sending out gunships to hit them."

"We need to get to the hospital and then take the strikers back to their camp. When that's done, Sergeant Fetterman and I want to take the prisoners into Saigon."

"Where?"

"Tan Son Nhut. The SOG building on the airport proper."

"I think we can do that."

Gerber nodded and retreated to the troop seat. He glanced at two of the Vietnamese strikers sitting there. One was dressed in Vietcong black and the other wore green fatigues with a black tiger-striped pattern. These strikers were good soldiers and had done all that was demanded of them. They hadn't slacked off when the patrol had spent days lying in the tall grass watching the Ho Chi Minh Trail. They had been as quiet and as still as Fetterman.

Gerber knew that some Vietnamese units threw away their rifles and ran when the first shots were fired. All of these men, though, had stood fast, firing at the enemy.

They didn't put out rounds just for the sake of shooting. Instead they made their bullets count.

He lifted a hand and wiped his face. Now that they were at fifteen hundred feet, the air was cooler and the sweat was beginning to dry. He glanced down at his hand, barely visible in the red lights of the chopper's interior, and saw that it was coated with grime. Days in the field did that.

Gerber turned his attention to the ground outside, now wrapped in darkness. A single light bobbed along in the blackness. He figured it was a lantern on an oxcart. Probably a farmer trying to get home before the VC and the Americans started their nightly cat-and-mouse game, which often killed civilians in cross fires.

Off in the distance he saw the glow of one of the huge American base camps. In Vietnam displaying a light usually invited an attack, except at the huge American camps. The camps were so big that Charlie's only response was to drop a few mortar rounds or rockets on them in the hope of causing some damage.

Gerber settled back, leaning against the gray soundproofing on the transmission wall. He closed his eyes, relaxing for the first time since the patrol had left the American camp near the Cambodian border. He was just beginning to realize that the pressure was off. They had gotten out safely.

Fetterman touched his knee, and when Gerber opened his eyes, the master sergeant shouted, "What's the drill now?"

"Into Tay Ninh to drop off the wounded and then back to the camp with the rest of the Vietnamese."

"Yes, sir," said Fetterman. "I understand that. I meant, what are we going to do then?"

"You have something on your mind, Master Sergeant?"

Fetterman glanced at the Vietnamese in the chopper. A noisy, open cargo compartment wasn't the place to hold a classified discussion. All he said was "I think we need to talk to Jerry Maxwell."

"Okay," said Gerber, closing his eyes again.

A moment later the noise of the Huey's turbine changed slightly, and Gerber felt the aircraft begin its descent. He opened his eyes. Outside was the huge base at Tay Ninh, parts of it looking as bright as it did during the day. The bunker line around the perimeter was dark, though the way the vegetation had been cut back for clean fields of fire marked it as clearly as if they had been lighted.

They crossed the perimeter, shot to a hover at the edge of the airfield and then taxied along the strip until they were close to the hospital. As they settled to the ground, the doors burst open and two men wheeling a gurney ran out. They veered toward the other chopper. In a moment they had the wounded man loaded and were taking him back into the hospital. A second crew collected the body of the dead man.

As the second group disappeared, they came up to a hover again, then took off, climbing upward parallel to the runway as they crossed the perimeter wire. Turning left, they kept climbing until they reached two thousand feet while still over Tay Ninh.

Gerber watched the landscape under him change as they headed out over thick jungle again. They reached the strikers' camp a few minutes later. It was an oval-shaped base with a runway outside the perimeter. There were sandbagged bunkers, a fire control tower in the middle of the camp near the commo bunker and the dispensary, a few small buildings and additional bunkers that served as living quarters. A hundred and fifty South Vietnamese lived there. The Americans were from the Twenty-fifth Infantry Division.

The choppers circled the camp once, then began a slow descent toward the end of the runway closest to the camp. They shot to a hover and kicked up a windstorm of red dust that obscured the camp until the choppers were on the ground and the rotors no longer moved.

The strikers leaped from the helicopters and ran for the camp. One American came out, glanced into the first chopper, then walked back to where Gerber and Fetterman waited. "How'd it go?" he asked.

"One dead and one wounded. We took out a patrol and bagged three prisoners."

"You can leave them here."

"No," said Gerber. "I want to take them into Saigon for interrogation."

"We have the capability."

"I know that," said Gerber. "I just want to have it done by our own men." He glanced at the other American. "No offense, but South Vietnamese interrogators sometimes get a little too enthusiastic in their work."

The men laughed. "I won't disagree with you there. Will you be coming back?"

"I don't know," said Gerber. "Depends on what we learn from the prisoners and what our debriefing determines." He hesitated, then added, "Oh, we need to have you debrief your strikers and send us a written report."

"No problem." The man held out his hand. "If you're ever back in the area, drop in."

"Certainly."

The man turned and hurried back toward the camp. As he did, the chopper came up to a hover, turned, then took off, heading for Saigon. Gerber sat back, but this time he watched the prisoners, who were now sitting with their backs against the rear of the armored seats used by the pilots. The three men watched Gerber, their eyes on his M-16. They looked as if they were afraid to move.

Fetterman slipped over and yelled, "They're not going to be happy in Saigon. They'll wonder why we had to bring the prisoners in tonight."

Gerber was silent for a moment, then said, "Fuck 'em. No one ever said this was supposed to be a nine-to-five war. They'll just have to do a little work this evening."

"And what are we going to do?"

"Once we unload the prisoners, I want to get downtown and grab a shower and some sleep."

"A nine-to-five war?"

"The difference, Tony, is that we've spent the past few days in the field. We deserve a little rest."

"Yes, sir. Just wanted to make sure we've got our priorities straight."

"We do."

4

DOWNTOWN SAIGON

Connel walked along the sidewalk, taking in the sights of Saigon and the odors of the city. The air stank of diesel fuel and car exhaust. But there was also the odor of humanity jammed into too small an area. Saigon was a city of two or three million, if refugees were counted, but it shouldn't have had more than five hundred thousand.

He stopped at a corner and looked down the street, a mirror image of what he had just passed. There were a dozen bars with bright neon, and Vietnamese women standing around, hoping a GI would strike up a conversation and spend some money on them.

But that wasn't the worst thing. Far worse was the line of so-called soldiers lining the street begging for money. Some of them were horribly mutilated, obviously the result of battle injuries. Others had faked their disabilities, playing on the sympathies of the Americans. It was just another way to separate the American soldier from the little money he was paid for his year in Vietnam.

Slowly Connel turned around, looking from the whores and cripples to the men and women circulating on the street. He shook his head and felt sick to his stomach. In that instant he hated everything about Vietnam. In that instant he knew he wasn't on a great adventure. There would be no glory in Vietnam. Only misery and death.

A woman approached him, grabbed his arm, then maneuvered herself around so that she was facing him. She pressed her body against his and then slipped a hand down to rub his crotch. "Hey, GI, you want to party?"

Connel looked down at her, ready to shove her aside as he had the others, but this time he didn't. Instead he gazed into her soft brown eyes. She had long black hair, a round face and looked as if she were no more than fifteen. He felt a stirring in his body, a sudden desire he wouldn't have thought possible. Maybe it was a chance to get even with the Vietnamese by using one of their women. Maybe it was just a desire to touch another human. He couldn't explain and didn't care to. All he knew was that he wanted this woman.

"How much?"

"One thousand P," she said. "Ten dollar. For a good time, only ten dollar."

"Too much. Five dollars."

"Okay, GI. You win."

Because she had given in too easily, Connel knew he was being taken. She grabbed his hand and pulled him toward the closest alley.

"Oh, no," said Connel. "I want to use a room. I'm not going to go on display like these others." His crotch was aching and his desire was almost crippling, but he wasn't going to succumb in an alley.

"You funny, GI."

He stared down at her. "You want the five bucks, you'll do it my way."

She nodded and pulled him along the sidewalk. They came to a hidden door, which she opened. Connel saw a dim light and a stairway that led up to the second floor. She pulled him up, but he wasn't sure he wanted to go. It was too dark at the top. Too dark and too lonely.

She led him down a hall that had one light at the far end. Everything was lost in shadows. The hallway stank of humidity, urine and vomit. And there was a musky smell that reminded him of sex.

They came to a door and she opened it. The room was small and the only light shone from the flashing neon outside. There was a mattress on the floor, the sheet pulled to one side. Near it was a small table holding a single candle. Next to a grimy window was a low bookcase with nothing in it.

As soon as they were inside, she began to tug at his clothes. First she tried to unbutton his shirt, then she started unzipping his pants. When she succeeded, she reached inside to grab him and found him ready for her. She squeezed gently. "You nice."

Connel felt his head swim. He wanted her badly. He touched her breasts. They were small, almost nonexistent. He fumbled with the buttons of her blouse, reached inside and found that her nipples were rockhard. He pinched one of them, and she moaned low in her throat.

Pulling him deeper into the room, she worked at the belt buckle and the button on his pants. She got them open and pushed the pants down around his ankles. Connel lifted his left foot free and with his right kicked them away. The woman pulled up her short skirt and revealed that she was wearing nothing under it.

Connel touched her and felt the soft, smooth skin of her thigh and then the sparse hair between her legs. Slowly he probed with a finger.

"Oh," she moaned, her voice suddenly husky. She pulled him toward the thin mattress and sat down. He stood over her, looking down. She reached up, grabbed him and then sat up, getting to her knees. She took him in her mouth, kissing and caressing.

Then there was a faint click behind Connel. He started to turn, but as he did, she flicked her tongue across his penis. He sucked in air and bit his lip.

The noise was repeated. It sounded as if someone was trying to open the door quietly. Again he tried to turn, but the woman squeezed tighter and used her tongue to drive all thoughts from his brain. She bobbed her head, moving her hand in time with her tongue, and Connel knew he was about to explode.

Out of the corner of his eye he saw a shadow flicker. The shadow crouched for a moment to one side, then slipped out of sight. He would have turned with it, trying to see it better, but his body was betraying him. He felt something build in the pit of his stomach, expand down into his crotch, and then suddenly he was groaning, his muscles tense and his eyes jammed shut.

Finished, he dropped to his knees. His breath rasped in his throat. He opened his eyes and looked at the woman. She had backed away from him and was working to adjust her clothes. She stood up, then ran to the door.

"Hey," yelled Connel, "where are you going?"

She opened the door and disappeared. Connel rolled onto his back and laughed. If she didn't want the money, he didn't care. That was up to her.

Finally he got up and moved to where his pants lay. He picked them up and put them on. Tucking his shirt in, he zipped up, buttoned up, then buckled his belt. Then, turning toward the window, he ran his hands through his hair to straighten it. Finally, reaching behind him, he touched his hip pocket. His wallet was gone!

"Son of a bitch! Son of a fucking bitch." He glanced at the floor but knew it wouldn't be there. That was the shadow he'd seen. That was why the woman had worked so hard to give him pleasure. She was diverting his attention so that he wouldn't be thinking about his wallet.

He leaped to the door and jerked it open. Close by he could hear the quiet thumping of two bodies as they worked on each other in another room. Music came from somewhere down the hall. Vietnamese music, not rock and roll. But there was no sign of the woman. She and her partner were gone.

Connel walked to the stairs and clambered down them. He stepped out into the street and watched the milling crowds, knowing that the woman was long gone. Hell, he wasn't sure he'd recognize her again even if she were right in front of him.

"Shit," he muttered, wondering how he was going to get back to the base. He had no idea where it was, how far away it was, or if he could find a ride with any of the military vehicles that still rumbled along the street.

"Welcome to Vietnam," he told himself.

THE PRISONERS DIDN'T MOVE during the forty-minute flight to Saigon. They sat rigidly, their backs against the armored pilot seats, and waited for something to happen to them. Gerber watched them carefully. Scared men sometimes made foolish moves because they figured there was nothing to lose. Enemy soldiers, told of torture at the hands of the Americans and the South Vietnamese, were sometimes frightened enough to be desperate. Gerber didn't want them to try anything at all.

Fetterman sat at the edge of the troop seat and watched the dark ground slip away under him. Then the door gunner leaned around from his well and yelled, "We're about ten minutes out."

"Did we get clearance into MACV-SOG at Tan Son Nhut?" asked Gerber.

"The AC wants to know where that is."

"Does he knew where the Air America pad is?"

The door gunner disappeared for a moment, then came back. "He says he does."

"Then he just needs to land at the next place beyond that. It's on the far side, away from Hotel Three."

"Got it," said the door gunner.

Fetterman leaned close. "There going to be anyone waiting for us?"

Gerber shrugged. "I imagine someone will be at the building."

"I meant someone to take the prisoners off our hands."

"We'll worry about that when we get there."

Looking through the windshield, Gerber saw they were getting close. Saigon, a golden glow that dominated the whole landscape, was spread out in front of them. To the right was Tan Son Nhut.

They entered the traffic pattern, slipped around and then lined up with the runway. Crossing over the Air America pad, they landed in front of a low one-story building. As the skids touched the tarmac, Gerber slipped to the right and got out.

Fetterman sat still, his eyes on the prisoners. Gerber walked around the front of the chopper and waited. Fetterman motioned to the prisoners. When they didn't move, he ordered them out in Vietnamese.

They moved closer to the building. The chopper then lifted, turned and took off. "You going to wait here, Tony?" asked Gerber.

"I can. What are you going to do?"

"Find someone to take charge of the prisoners and get them over to the prison compound," said Gerber. "Then we're out of here."

"Shouldn't we write our reports, let Maxwell know we're back and alert command that we're available if they need us for anything?"

"Of course," said Gerber. "Instead we'll find someone to hand these prisoners over to and then we're on our way downtown. Tomorrow's soon enough for everything else."

Fetterman shook his head. "I think the whole world's going to hell in a hand basket."

"Well," said Gerber, "if you feel that strongly about it, then we'll do it your way."

"Let's not get ridiculous, sir. I didn't say I wasn't in the hand basket."

Gerber moved to the front door of the SOG building. It had once been an open screen, but then someone had bought an air conditioner so the door had been covered with clear plastic, which the tropical air, humidity and grime had soon turned milky white. Gerber opened the door and entered the short, narrow hall.

To the right was a dayroom that contained a broken-down couch, a card table with four wooden chairs around it and a refrigerator that normally contained Coke and beer and sometimes the makings of a sandwich or two. Beyond the dayroom, farther down the hall, was a radio room. Opposite it was a planning room and then a warehouse that held weapons, uniforms and supplies from nearly every country in the world.

Two NCOs were in the dayroom. One of them wore jungle pants, an OD T-shirt that was ripped and jungle boots that weren't laced. The other man was stretched out on the couch, asleep.

"Either of you busy?" asked Gerber.

"No, sir," the sergeant with the torn OD T-shirt answered.

"I need someone to take a couple of prisoners over to the compound."

The man bent over and began lacing his boots. "I'll take them."

"I appreciate it. My sergeant and I have been in the field and we'd like to get downtown."

"Give me a couple of minutes."

"Fine. Tell them we'll be by tomorrow to see how things are going and to ask a few questions. And then take a beer out of petty cash for yourself."

"Thank you, sir."

Gerber went outside. He stood there for a moment, wishing he was already downtown. He wished he'd already had a shower and was sitting down to eat a giant meal, complete with a bottle of wine.

As he approached, Fetterman asked, "Did you call Miss Morrow to let her know we're back in town?"

"Not yet."

The sergeant from the dayroom appeared. He had found a pistol belt with a .45 hanging on it and was carrying an M-16. "Ready, Captain."

"Thanks again," said Gerber.

The man pointed at the prisoners and ordered, "Move it out."

As the sergeant marched them down the road behind the Air America hangar, Fetterman asked, "You didn't locate a jeep for us, did you, Captain?"

"Figured we'd just grab a cab."

Fetterman shook his head. "Sometimes I don't know about officers. They're supposed to be so smart. You guys run the army and design programs for the enlisted troops, but you don't know how to promote a ride."

"It's no problem."

"That's because you're with me. Come on."

Fetterman led Gerber across the road to where there were half a dozen jeeps parked. The master sergeant crouched and reached up over the right rear wheel. He held up a small black box and smiled. "Key. Shall we go?"

Gerber put his M-16 into the back and climbed into the passenger seat. "There a key in every jeep in this parking lot?"

"No, sir. Just a couple of them."

"Shit," he said. "It figures that all you NCOs take care of one another."

Fetterman got behind the wheel. He used the key to unlock the padlock on the chain looped through the wheel and bolted to the floor. A thief could start the engine but not turn the wheels. He dropped the chain and lock out of the way and started the jeep. Before backing out, he asked, "If we don't take care of one another, who's going to do it?"

"I haven't the faintest idea."

"Precisely." He twisted around, backed up, then shifted into first. "Where to?"

"The hotel, of course. We need to clean up. Then we'll get something to eat."

"Sounds good to me."

NO ONE IN THE HOTEL LOBBY seemed concerned about seeing two dirty, armed men walk through. No one cared when they went up to the reservations desk and collected keys for the rooms they kept at the hotel even when they were in the field. Keys in hand, Fetterman and Gerber headed straight for the elevator, waited and then stepped into it. It was a gilded cage that allowed them to look down into the lobby as it made its way up into the hotel.

The lobby was an expanse of marble with Victorian furniture scattered here and there. A dozen people milled around the teak registration desk. But Gerber didn't pay much attention to the lobby. He'd seen it innumerable times. Finally the elevator reached the third floor and Gerber stepped out. "Meet you in thirty minutes in the restaurant."

"Yes, sir. You going to call Miss Morrow?"

"You've got a one-track mind, Tony. I'll call Robin in the morning. Tonight I just want to eat and sleep."

"Yes, sir." The elevator door closed and Fetterman vanished.

Gerber walked down the hall, feeling out of place. There was still mud from Cambodia on his boots and his uniform was filthy and torn in several places. He was still wearing his rucksack and pistol belt and had his M-16 in one hand. His whole body ached for a shower and a big meal.

When he reached his door, he used his key and opened the louvered door. The room was dark except for a bit of light bleeding in from the street below. Red and blue neon flashed from the bar signs outside. He reached around and snapped on the overhead light. Something stirred near his bed and Gerber automatically dropped to one knee, bringing his rifle up quickly, his thumb snapping off the safety.

"Hey, Mack."

Slowly Gerber got to his feet, releasing the pressure on the trigger. His heart hammered in his chest and his blood surged through his veins. Lowering his rifle, he said, "Evening, Robin. What are you doing here?"

"Hiding out." She sat up on his bed, and the sheet that had been covering her fell away. She wasn't wearing much.

Gerber reached behind him and closed the door. With his left hand he locked it, then moved deeper into the room. He walked over to a chair near the window and sat down.

"Didn't expect you tonight," she said. "You scared the hell out of me."

Gerber propped his rifle in the corner behind the chair, unbuckled his pistol belt, leaned forward and shrugged his way out of his rucksack. Twisting, he set it on the floor by the chair, then reached up under his jungle jacket to remove the Browning M-35 pistol concealed there.

"I thought carrying a concealed weapon was against regulations," Morrow said.

"It is," replied Gerber. "Stupid regulation, isn't it?"

"I suppose."

Gerber leaned back and rubbed his face, then stared at Morrow. "Why are you hiding out?"

"No real reason. I just didn't want them to be able to find me tonight. I wanted a good night's sleep without some dummy calling with what he thought was the world's greatest story. I didn't think you'd be back. I guess I won't be getting much sleep, after all.''

"Let me get a shower and we'll see about that."

Now she grinned broadly. "What about Sergeant Fetterman?"

Gerber didn't say a word.

"Come on, Mack. I know the two of you. You've got something going on for this evening."

"Just something to eat. I'm supposed to meet him in the restaurant."

"And if you don't show?"

"He'll order his own dinner, eat it and then go to bed. He's a big boy."

"So what are you going to do?"

Gerber stared at her long light brown hair, which had been bleached blond by the tropical sun. A few bangs brushed her green eyes. She had a tanned, angular face that made her look gaunt. The rest of her body was white. The contrast between her arms and face and her chest was startling. The skin looked impossibly white. Finally he said, "I think I'll take a shower and then we'll consider our options."

"And Sergeant Fetterman?"

"He can think up his own fun."

5

TAN SON NHUT
SAIGON

Connel woke up in a foul mood. He'd slept on top of his cot, sweating heavily in the late-night heat. There was no air-conditioning and he hadn't been able to get a fan. He'd had to stay in the stifling room, the windows open and hope for a cool breeze, and although the wind had picked up, it was hot and humid and just made everything seem even hotter.

He sat up and felt his head spin. He'd had too much to drink after the bitch had stolen his wallet. Other soldiers, both Army and Air Force, had bought him beer when they found out what had happened to him. All claimed that it had happened to them or to friends, and all had learned to keep their wallets close to them if they were in a room with a South Vietnamese national. Now Connel knew why some soldiers didn't mind standing in an alley. That way the whore's accomplice couldn't get close enough to steal anything. Not with an audience watching.

It wasn't the money that bothered Connel. He'd been smart enough to leave most of it in his room. What really steamed him was all the stuff he'd have to replace, starting with his ID card. There would be some laughs at PASS and ID when he told them he'd lost his ID card.

He stood up and walked to the window. A light haze hugged the ground, making it seem as if the sky were sweating. Feeling miserable and hating Vietnam more than he'd ever hated anything, Connel found his shaving kit and an OD towel and walked out of the room clad only in his shorts. His dog tags jangled as he walked down the hall in his bare feet. He hadn't had the energy to dig through his duffel bag in search of his shower shoes.

The shower room was separated from his quarters by a dozen yards. Connel didn't care if anyone saw him walk into it wearing so little. He found that he cared about nothing at all except the 363 days and a wake-up before he could go home.

He left his shaving kit on a sink, hung his towel on a hook, took off his shorts and entered the shower room. There were sheet metal walls, a latticework of thin wood on the floor for drainage and screens near the top to let the breezes in and the moisture out. The rafters were open so that he could look up at the corrugated tin roof.

Turning on the water, he was surprised by the tepid spray. He jumped back, but then the flow faded to a miserable trickle. Connel stood under it, turning slowly, trying to get wet. He soaped, rinsed and got out to dry himself. Finally he shaved, wrapped his towel around his waist and trudged back to his room.

He put on a clean fatigue uniform and new jungle boots and left for the eight-o'clock class the sergeant had told him about yesterday. When he arrived, he stood there for a moment, the sweat already staining his fatigues, and wished he had been smarter in college. He'd been swayed by the promise of fifty dollars a month in pay for attending ROTC classes, and fifty dollars a month bought a lot of beer. He hadn't counted on a trip to Vietnam being a booby prize. At least not until his senior year, when the handwriting on the wall became obvious.

GERBER MET FETTERMAN in the lobby of the hotel. The master sergeant was standing at the windows, looking out onto the street. Hordes of people still circulated out there. Saigon never let up. Something was always going on. Fetterman saw Gerber's approaching reflection in the glass and turned. "Morning, Captain. I missed you at dinner last night."

"Couldn't be avoided," said Gerber.

"Yes, sir. What's the plan for today?"

Gerber looked at his watch. He was hungry, having failed to eat the night before and having already missed breakfast. "I think we should head over to MACV and see what Maxwell has to tell us."

"And to round up some doughnuts?" asked Fetterman.

"Well, there is that, I suppose."

Fetterman moved toward the door. A Vietnamese leaped forward and opened it for him. Gerber followed the master sergeant down to the street, surprised at how hot it was. Sweat beaded immediately, and the captain glanced up at the morning sky. "It's going to be a hot one."

Fetterman didn't respond, and together they walked toward the jeep that Fetterman had driven the night before. As the master sergeant unlocked the steering wheel, Gerber climbed into the passenger seat.

Wiping the sweat from his face, Gerber said, "Once we're done with Maxwell, let's drive over and see what's become of our prisoners."

Fetterman started the engine. "Yes, sir."

He pulled out into the traffic. Gerber leaned back and put a foot on the dashboard. He watched as the traffic thinned slightly and then filled in around them. Fetterman worked his way through the Lambrettas, bicycles, trucks and cars and turned a corner onto a wide street where the traffic thinned considerably. They drove down it and passed a sandbagged bunker with a tank sitting in front of it.

Turning again, they pulled into the gravel parking lot outside of MACV headquarters, stopping at a white chain erected on poles to mark the perimeter. Fetterman and Gerber got out and walked past the double flagpoles that were surrounded by flowers. They reached the double doors of the building and entered. As they did, the cold air from the interior rolled out and washed over them. Gerber was always surprised about that. It seemed ridiculous to waste so much energy to keep the interior of a building so cold.

They entered a hallway lined with posters warning soldiers to watch out for the enemy, to safeguard classified information, to wear the uniform properly and to stay away from the local women. Passing a T-intersection, they descended a flight of stairs. When they reached the bottom, they found a wrought iron gate guarded by an MP armed with an M-16. The soldier stood up as Gerber and Fetterman approached.

"Yes, sir?"

"Like to see Jerry Maxwell."

"Name?"

"Captain Gerber and Sergeant Fetterman."

The MP consulted a list, ran his finger down it until he found their names, then said, "Yes, sir. Sign in with your name, date and time."

Gerber and Fetterman complied, then the guard asked to see their ID cards just to be sure. Satisfied, he opened the gate and let them through.

They walked down another tiled hallway. Rust spots where filing cabinets and metal bookcases had stood stained the floor. The cinder block walls were beaded with moisture. Finally they came to Maxwell's door, which wasn't marked. Gerber knocked, waited, then knocked again.

"Hold your fucking water," said a muffled voice from inside. An instant later the door opened and Maxwell appeared. "What the fuck do you want?"

"Very nice, Jerry," said Gerber evenly. "We drive all the way over here to visit with you and you give us a ration of shit."

"Just come on in and sit down." Maxwell retreated into his office and sat down at his desk, which was cluttered with a mountain of paper. Empty Coke cans lined the side of the desk next to the cinder block wall. A visitor's chair and a row of filing cabinets completed the basic office furniture.

Gerber took the chair, sat down and relaxed. Fetterman closed the door and then moved toward the corner so that he could lean against the filing cabinet. He picked at the blizzard of paper piled on top of them.

Maxwell closed a file folder that had Secret stamped on the top and bottom and stuffed it into his desk drawer. Then he turned and faced Gerber. The CIA man didn't look good. He'd been in Vietnam for a long time, and since he wasn't part of the military, he didn't have the luxury of a preprogrammed date to return home. He stayed on until the CIA decided he had either screwed up so badly they had to get rid of him or that he had functioned so brilliantly that he deserved a reward.

As a result of the tension, Maxwell was a thin man. His white suit hung on his bony frame and his black hair had thinned and was slicked down. There were dark circles around his eyes and an unhealthy pallor to his skin. His hands were shaking as he pushed the report out of sight.

"You okay, Jerry?" asked Gerber.

"I'm fine. Tired. Just very tired."

"Maybe it's time you took a vacation," said Fetterman.

"We don't take vacations," said Maxwell. "There's too much to do for a vacation."

Gerber glanced at Fetterman and shrugged. He turned back to Maxwell. "Thought you'd want to know what we saw along the Ho Chi Minh Trail."

"Doesn't matter," said Maxwell.

Gerber again looked at Fetterman. He felt anger course through him. They'd spent the time in the field, in Cambodia, waiting for the enemy to jump them. One man had been killed and another wounded. Now Maxwell was dismissing the patrol as if it were no more than a walk in the park.

"What in hell do you mean?" asked Fetterman. The anger was unmistakable in his voice.

Maxwell lifted a hand and waved it. "I mean, that a new wrinkle has been added."

"We learned some very interesting things out there," said Gerber.

"What?"

"For one thing, traffic on the Trail is way down. Only a few men and supplies are moving along it, not the river of supplies that used to be flowing down it before Tet."

"Hell, I could have told you that," said Maxwell.

"No, Jerry," said Fetterman. "You could have told us that you suspected it, but you couldn't have told us that it was happening until we went out and looked."

"So what?" asked Maxwell.

"Shit!" snapped Gerber. "It was your idea that we go out there in the first place."

Again Maxwell raised his hand. "Intelligence work is the gathering of information from as many sources as possible so that we have a complete picture."

"I don't need a short course on intelligence work," said Gerber.

"My point is simply that, with what we've learned through those other sources, we now have a clear picture of what's happening."

"Even without debriefing us?" asked Gerber.

"You already told me all I have to know. Traffic has slowed way down on the trail. That confirms what we already know."

"So what does it mean?" asked Fetterman.

"Charlie, the North Vietnamese, have infiltrated everyone they want in the South. They now have everything they need in place."

"Meaning?" Gerber asked.

"They'll launch their attack soon."

CONNEL HAD BEEN QUIET through the earlier session, listening to a sergeant tell him what it was like in Vietnam. He hadn't pointed out that all of them, the men in the folding chairs and those standing in front of them, had all been through the same training. The only difference was that the men in front had been in Vietnam for a couple of months. Now they were talking as if they had years of combat experience.

That session ended and they were given a break. Connel watched as a Vietnamese kid carrying a metal ammo box walked through the crowd, selling ice-cold Coke. Connel watched a sergeant buy one, haggling with the kid for a few seconds and then giving him a couple of small bills, quarters or dimes made of paper rather than coins.

"Hey, kid," yelled Connel, "over here."

The Vietnamese boy looked and then picked up his ammo case. He walked over, set it down and opened it. "You want Coke? Fifty cents."

"I'm not paying fifty cents for a Coke."

"Fifty cents."

"I'll give you a quarter."

The kid nodded. "A quarter for Coke. A quarter for bottle."

Connel took a deep breath, but then said nothing. He pulled the MPC out and handed it over. The kid stuffed the money into the pocket of his ragged pants, pulled a bottle from the ammo can and used the opener that was on a chain around his neck. Then he handed the open bottle to Connel.

As the kid began to work the rest of the crowd, Connel took a drink. The Coke tasted funny. It wasn't the sweet nectar he was used to. It seemed flatter somehow, almost like colored dirty water.

"Hey," he said.

One of the sergeants said, "They don't use the same formula at the bottling plant here."

"They've got a bottling plant in Saigon?"

"Hell, Lieutenant, Coke's everywhere." He laughed. "Soldiers and politicians fight over land, and when the war's over the corporations who made money on the war are the only ones left. The soldiers and the politicians are all gone.''

Connel tried the Coke again. He didn't like it and wouldn't have finished it if it hadn't been wet and cold. He tilted the bottle and swallowed rapidly.

"You don't like it," said the sergeant, "then you have to stick with the PX. They got all the Coke you need, and it was all made in the World."

Connel nodded and started to throw the bottle away.

"Hey," said the sergeant, "use your head, man. The kid charged you a fucking quarter for the bottle. You toss it aside, the kid picks it up and has an extra quarter. Sell it back to him."

"Fuck it," said Connel. He threw the bottle at the ground, where it shattered. "There. Now he can't get it back and sell it for another quarter."

The sergeant looked at the bits of glass and shook his head. "Now somebody's going to have to pick that up."

"Probably be some Vietnamese, so fuck him, too."

When the break was over, they were put on a bus, again with thick screens over the windows, armed guards at the doors and sheet metal over part of the windshield. They drove away from Tan Son Nhut, hit a highway and headed north. As they left the city, Connel was surprised. He'd thought of Vietnam as a backward country, and once they were out of Saigon, he expected nothing more than jungles and rice paddies. But they were driving along a modern four-lane highway, with no sign of jungle anywhere. There was a hill to the west that swept upward gently with an abstract sculpture perched at the top. Someone told him it was a cemetery for South Vietnamese soldiers killed in the war.

They crossed a bridge that looked as if it had been opened earlier that day, then continued on until they came to the gate of another American base. The bus slowed, but the MP at the gate, dressed in jungle fatigues and a flak jacket and holding an M-16 in his left hand, waved them through.

They diverted to a dirt road near the perimeter. On the right were bunkers made of the green rubberized sandbags he was seeing everywhere. A skeleton crew manned them in case of a daylight attack. But no one expected an assault because there were too many Americans at the camp and any attack would quickly turn into a funeral for the enemy.

They turned again and stopped at an outdoor classroom. Bleachers sat in the little shade afforded by young trees that might be more useful in another twenty years. In front of the bleachers was a mock-up of an American perimeter. Two sergeants, both in jungle fatigues, stood off to one side. A Vietnamese dressed only in black shorts stood with them.

The men filtered out of the bus and spread out on the bleachers. Connel sat at one end in the partial shade of a palm and looked at the ground in front of him. It had the look of a desert. The vegetation had been killed by Agent Orange and the trampling feet of thousands of men who had been herded to the bleachers for the show the two sergeants had prepared.

When everyone was seated, one of the sergeants moved so that he was centered in front of the group. "Gentlemen," he said, "my name is Sergeant Chavez and this block of instruction is designed to teach you about the abilities of the Vietcong. We're going to show you that no matter how safe you feel inside your camp with its rows of concertina, barbed wire, claymores and trip flares, you are *not* safe."

He gestured at the concertina-and-bunker mock-up that stood there. "This is actually in better shape than most of what you'll find in the field. Sergeant Thomsen and I built it carefully, constructing it according to various operations manuals and the current wisdom on the subject." He moved closer. "We have extra tanglefoot at the base. There's extra wire strung through the concertina and there are two dozen extra cans on the wire."

He held up a Budweiser can. "This little trick sometimes works." He shook the can, and the stone in it rattled. "Charlie touches the wrong wire and the can rattles, alerting you." He crouched and pointed. "Trip flares here and here and here." He gestured broadly. "More scattered through the perimeter."

He stood up and rubbed the dust off his palms. Pointing, he said, "We've got claymores there and there. Command-detonated and rigged with trip wires. Every defensive measure has been taken." He looked up at the men in the bleachers. "Anyone have any suggestions or ideas? Anything that we might have missed?"

He waited, but no one spoke. "We've done it all here. Got it all here. An impenetrable defense." The Vietnamese moved forward, as if on cue. Chavez clapped him on the shoulder. "Okay, Nguyen, show them your stuff."

The Vietnamese crouched, then stretched out on his back. He slipped under the first strand of wire, twisted around and then began to work his way through the booby-trapped, trip-flared barricade. He worked rapidly, disconnecting the booby traps without rocking the cans. Pushing on through, he turned the claymores around so that they were facing the bunkers and then worked his way back out. The whole demonstration took no more than five minutes.

Chavez took center stage again. He waved at the concertina and then at Nguyen. "Any questions?"

Connel stood up. "That's an easy trick in the daylight. He can see everything and knows what to touch and what to leave alone."

Now Chavez grinned. It was as if it were all planned. Thomsen moved forward and pulled a blindfold from the left pocket of his jungle jacket. He snapped it open and tied it over Nguyen's eyes.

The Vietnamese dropped to the ground and felt his way along it. He reached the wire, and then using only his sense of touch, worked his way from one end of the mock perimeter to the other. He wasn't as quick as the first time, but he completed his task without making a sound.

"Jesus!" said one of the men, whistling.

Chavez nodded. "That's only for starters. It teaches you that you have to check the perimeter regularly, you can't go to sleep for a moment, and that enemy soldiers are experts at infiltration techniques. More than once men on a perimeter have gone out the next morning to find the claymores have been turned."

"So what?" said Connel. "They're inside bunkers. Even if they pop them, the damage will be to the sandbags. Our people will survive."

Chavez shook his head. "But if you're about to be overrun and you figure the claymores are the ace in the hole, then you're fucked, even if you survive the blast. A weapon pointed back at you doesn't do shit for you. Especially with Charlie in the wire, trying to kill your ass."

Connel nodded, realizing the sergeant was right. He wondered why he was so obsessed with this. He didn't want the Vietnamese to be good at anything. And then he realized that's exactly what it was. He didn't want to admit the VC could sneak into an American camp easily. He didn't want to believe the enemy could defeat American expertise and technology. Not easily, anyway.

"The lesson to be learned here," said Chavez, "is that we have to be better than the enemy. We can't sit back and think he's a dumbass not worthy of thought. Charlie's a wily bastard who'll kill you if you give him half a chance. My job is to teach you enough so that you don't give him that half a chance."

Connel nodded. The lesson wouldn't be lost on him. Give Charlie a chance and he'd kill you.

6

BANG RON REPUBLIC OF VIETNAM

Gerber, having learned nothing from the prisoners, sat in what would have been the team house had it been a Special Forces camp. It was a small room, half buried in the soft red dirt of South Vietnam and no more than twenty miles from Cambodia. The furnishings, what little there were, had been stolen or built by the men of the camp. There were a couple of lawn chairs, the fabric beginning to fray badly. There was one card table that wobbled and another table built of second-rate pine. Along one wall were shelves made from bricks and wood torn from ammo boxes. They held canned goods. There was a bar across the back end of the room, and behind it were liquor bottles and cases of Coke and beer.

Sitting across from him was a first lieutenant, Richard Suttin, who didn't look more than twenty or twenty-one. He wore mud-stained jungle fatigues and there was a light peach fuzz on his face that matched his blond hair. Like nearly everyone in Vietnam, his skinny face had taken on the appearance of a skull. The skin was taut and there were black rings around his eyes. But it was a healthy-looking skull with a deep tropical tan.

In front of them, sitting on the table, were two cans of Coke. Suttin took a drink from his can and set it down. "I don't understand why you're back here."

"We heard you were having some trouble with the enemy," Gerber said. "Sporadic contact?"

"I'm not sure what you'd call it. We've run into the VC a couple of times, but each time we do they break the contact immediately and retreat."

Gerber stared at the younger man. "You think that's significant?"

"Yes, sir. Here's why. In the past we've had similar things happen—contact with Charlie bugging out. But sometimes he'd stand and fight. If we were about equally matched, or if he had us outnumbered, he'd fight. Now he always runs."

"Regardless of odds?"

"Regardless of odds or the time of day or the terrain. Nothing makes any difference to him. He always wants to break contact."

"I want to take out a patrol," Gerber said. "Sergeant Fetterman will accompany me, and I'd like to take twelve, maybe fifteen of your strikers."

Suttin hesitated, then nodded. "Hell, Captain, I'm happy for any help you can give us." He grinned. "It's just one less patrol I have to do."

"I'd like to get out about noon, spend the night in the field and come in either tomorrow or the next day."

Suttin finished his Coke. "Sure. The one thing I don't understand is why you're here."

"Doing my job," said Gerber. "Gathering intelligence so the paper pushers in Saigon will have a reason to push all those papers around."

Suttin stood. "Let's go take a look around."

"Certainly."

LITTLE MORE THAN AN HOUR later Fetterman stood at the edge of the camp, a row of Vietnamese strikers in front of him. He moved along the row slowly, glancing at each man. They all had M-16s, which was unusual for the South Vietnamese. Normally they were armed with a variety of weapons, most of which had gone out of style twenty years earlier. Each of them had a rucksack that contained C-rations, clean socks, a first aid kit and spare ammo. Each man had something that was considered squad equipment. One might have spare batteries for the radio or spare ammo for the M-79 or the M-60. One might be carrying extra flares or a survival radio.

Fetterman inspected the men carefully, making sure their weapons and ammo were clean and that they hadn't replaced the heavy batteries with lightweight dummies. After having worked with the men on a couple of other patrols, he expected them to be top-notch. But he also knew that the minute he slacked off, they would, too, and in combat that could get them all killed.

Gerber approached and Fetterman came to attention. He didn't salute, knowing Gerber didn't like to be identified as an officer in case there was a sniper in the area.

"Relax, Sergeant. How do they look?"

"Everything's ready, sir. Whenever you're ready to take off."

"About ten minutes," said Gerber. He pulled a map from his pocket and opened it.

Fetterman moved closer. He glanced over Gerber's shoulder at the camp. It had a small perimeter so that firepower could be concentrated no matter where the enemy attacked. There were mortar pits, but only three of them, a Browning M-2 fifty-caliber machine gun commanding each approach. In short, the camp was small but easily defensible, unless Charlie decided he wanted it badly enough to sacrifice a regiment.

Gerber pointed at the center of the map, where the camp was. "To the north here, first along this stream and then upward to this ridge line. From there we should be able to see out into this valley."

"Yes, sir," Fetterman said, lowering his voice. "You sure this is what Maxwell was hinting at? I hate it when he gets clever. Too many ways to misinterpret what he wants."

Gerber folded the map and tucked it away. "I'm as sure as I can be. He was obviously steering us here, and his comments about no longer needing our intelligence were designed to make us look harder for the enemy. I think he wants to know where some of those troop concentrations are."

Fetterman nodded. "If we run into them, there isn't a thing we can do. Not with a patrol this size."

"I know, but Charlie would tumble to a company-sized patrol, and its chances of survival aren't any better."

"Jesus," said Fetterman. "I wish I believed this trip was necessary."

THE POINT MAN RAN through the gate, across the hard-packed dirt of the airstrip and into the elephant grass on the other side. He slowed there, walking carefully, trying to avoid the razor-sharp edges of the grass. Then he turned slightly, more toward the north, and headed for the trees.

Gerber watched him go, and then the rest of the patrol wormed its way out through the flimsy gate made of old two-by-fours and barbed wire. Gerber thought about all the times he'd watched Fetterman leave with a patrol. They'd had their own camp and their own strikers, and Gerber had known the capability of the patrol. Here they were working with borrowed assets, and that could spell disaster.

As the last striker left, Gerber fell in behind him. He walked across the airfield, looking at the hard-packed red dirt filled with tiny, flinty stones that could cut the hell out of tires, boot soles or bare feet. When he got to the elephant grass, he followed the path marked by the front of the patrol. There were two reasons for that. One was that elephant grass was tough to walk through. A soldier had to be careful: the grass could easily rip his leather boots. And the second reason was that Gerber knew the path contained no booby traps: a trip wire or a pressure plate would have been exposed by now.

Even with that, Gerber scanned the ground in front of him, looking for evidence of a booby trap, and then farther out, right and left, searching for signs of an ambush. Finally he glanced at the trees in the distance, again trying to spot something that didn't belong, trying to see the enemy before they saw him.

Halfway across the field he was bathed in sweat. The sun beat down mercilessly and baked the ground. To the west were thunderheads that threatened rain later. But now it was just hot and humid.

They reached the trees and filtered into them, spreading out in a ring. Fetterman was at the center, waiting for him. Gerber crouched near the master sergeant.

"Ten minutes, Captain, and then we're off again."

"It's good to get out of the sun. Might make things a little easier."

"Might," said Fetterman. "Heading still the same?"

"Just along the stream. Keep it in sight, but we don't want to walk along the bank."

"No, sir."

Gerber rubbed the back of his neck, surprised at how wet it was. He knelt with one knee on the carpet of rotting vegetation, pulled out a canteen and took a drink, sloshing the water around in his mouth before swallowing it. Then he capped the canteen and put it away.

He wished he had listened to Robin the night before. She had told him to stay away from Maxwell, otherwise he'd end up in the field somewhere. But here he was again, looking for solid evidence that Charlie and the North Vietnamese were building up their strength. Maxwell didn't want more speculation based on limited observation; he wanted proof.

"We're ready to go, sir," said Fetterman.

Gerber nodded. From that moment on he'd have to keep his mind on the task at hand. It might be pleasant to think of Robin lying on his bed, wearing nothing but a light coat of perspiration, but that kind of thinking could make him careless. Concentration was the key to surviving in the jungle.

Fetterman, accompanied by one of the strikers, moved off to the north. As they disappeared into the trees, the rest of the patrol began to move, Gerber bringing up the rear.

They moved through a jungle that was little more than a forest. Some ground clutter, ferns, bushes and saplings, covered every square inch of ground. Dead leaves, rotting vegetation and decaying animals formed a wet, stinking carpet.

But as they moved deeper into the jungle, the vegetation became denser. Bamboo grew in thick clumps.

Wait-a-minute vines hung everywhere. And the canopy overhead became an interwoven blanket that let in little sunlight.

Looking to the left, Gerber saw something slide along a low-hanging branch. From the shape of the head and the color of the body, black and yellow, Gerber knew it was a krait, one of the deadliest snakes in the world. It's poison worked in a matter of seconds and could easily kill a man. Warily Gerber watched the serpent slip to the ground and vanish into the bushes. He was surprised to see such a nocturnal creature in the daytime. Still, he wished he hadn't seen it at all. Kraits were bad news.

Keeping his eyes moving, he looked for other snakes. Then he remembered that some snakes draped themselves over branches so that they could bite anything moving down a trail. The jungle was infested with snakes. And there were spiders that seemed large enough to drag off a man. Centipedes were also a problem. Their poisonous bites might not be deadly, but they could make life miserable for a couple of days.

Finally the patrol reached the stream, then moved back deeper into the jungle. Through gaps in the vegetation, Gerber saw the water sparkling in the patchwork of sunlight filtering through the canopy above it.

They halted for a moment and spread out in a loose ring so that they could watch one another's back. Gerber examined his map, not sure where they were. Landmarks in the jungle were difficult to find. The stream was one. An outcropping of rock spiraling upward two or three hundred feet would have been another, but he couldn't see it. The jungle was too dense. He did know they were climbing slightly, heading up the first of the hills that separated them from the valley. They had gotten there faster than he'd thought they would.

Fetterman moved the men out again. The pace slowed, partly because the jungle had gotten so thick that it was difficult to move quickly without hacking, and partly because Fetterman was searching for the enemy. Speed had killed more than one soldier.

They climbed steadily, the rise in the ground becoming more pronounced. The soft carpet began to take on rough spots. Rocks stuck up through the ground. Some were small stones that could be kicked aside. Others were boulders that would have to be blasted clear if someone wanted to move them.

To the right there was a steep cliff of weathered gray rock. A few trees grew from cracks, and some vines hung from the top, looking like ropes thrown down by mountain climbers. Gerber could hear the crashing of a waterfall nearby. He remembered seeing that on the map, or rather the indications of it. Steep terrain lines suggested a cliff and the path of the stream suggested a waterfall. They were on the right course.

When they reached the top of the hill, they fanned out again. Gerber, bent nearly double so that he didn't expose himself against the tree-studded skyline, worked his way forward. Fetterman knelt behind a tree trunk, his right hand on a gray-green boulder.

Gerber slipped to the ground next to the master sergeant. The trees and bushes fell away abruptly, giving him a terrific view of the valley below. There was a sea of green treetops with a break that marked the path of the river. Here and there he could see slashes, the result of B-52 strikes or artillery bombardment. White wisps of moisture drifted near the tops of the trees so that it looked as if part of the jungle were on fire.

"There's the valley, Captain."

"We got here much sooner than I thought we would."

"Map's not that accurate," said Fetterman. "You'd think with satellites, U-2s and recon flights they could get us some good maps."

"You'd think," said Gerber. He pulled out his binoculars and swept the area slowly, searching for something that was marked on the map. "Nothing."

"We'll have to go down," said Fetterman. "They could hide a division under those trees."

Gerber lowered his binoculars. "I figured that if we could see anything from up here, then the Air Force could have seen it and Maxwell wouldn't have wanted us to come out and take a personal look."

"Kind of what I thought, too."

"So," asked Gerber, "how do you want to handle this?"

Fetterman pulled at his lips with his right hand. Then he wiped his fingers on his sweat-soaked fatigues. "You and me go down tonight and look around. The strikers stay put here as a rear guard. We get into trouble, and they cause a diversion so we can get out."

"Okay," said Gerber nodding. "I thought you'd want something like that."

"You objecting, Captain?"

"No. I'm just not dancing, either."

"Tonight, then?" asked Fetterman.

"Just after sunset. We might have to stay down there tomorrow, hiding out."

"Better recon that way."

"All right," said Gerber. "Let's get the strikers briefed and then I want to get some rest."

"Yes, sir. And we'll move out just after dusk?"

"Afraid so."

7

BIEN HOA, RVN

The classes ended, and when they did, Sergeant Chavez said, ''Before loading the bus to return to Saigon, we have orders for some of you. You'll be moving out to your operational units in the morning.''

Connel sat quietly, hoping his name was on the list, because he didn't want to waste any more time listening to former Vietcong tell him everything the Americans did wrong in Vietnam. He didn't want to sit through any more classes that told him the things he had learned before climbing on the airplane to fly across the big pond.

Then he heard his name called and he held up his right hand. Chavez moved toward him slowly and handed him the envelope that contained his orders. Connel ripped it open and extracted the four sheets of paper. He saw that he was assigned to the Twenty-fifth Infantry Division, Third Brigade, with headquarters at Tay Ninh. He was to report as early as possible in the morning.

With the orders handed out, the men climbed back onto the bus and waited for the driver, who had gotten lost somewhere on the base. He finally appeared, and without a word, climbed behind the wheel. As they rolled out the gate, Connel closed his eyes and fell asleep.

An hour later the bus stopped in front of his quarters at Tan Son Nhut. He climbed out and walked to his room, oblivious to the stale odor and heat. Opening the door to his room, he found that it had been cleaned and straightened by someone.

He knew he couldn't expect any mail for two weeks, but he found himself wishing for some. Sitting down on the cot, he looked at the dirty plywood floor. "Shit," he muttered. No one had told him what to do about dinner, what to do about entertainment that night, and no one had told him how he was supposed to get to Tay Ninh.

Thinking about it, he knew getting to Tay Ninh would be the easiest of his problems. He'd just ask base operations in the morning and someone would give him the information. But that was tomorrow's problem.

He took off his uniform and dropped it onto the floor. Then he pulled a towel from the rack above the cot and wiped the sweat off his body. Figuring the odds were long that he could find the Vietnamese woman who had robbed him the night before, he still decided it wouldn't hurt to look. He dressed in his civilian clothes, took some money, stuffed it into his sock and left everything else hidden in his room.

Getting downtown was no problem. Once again he argued with the taxi driver about the price of the ride, finally giving him a buck and a half and telling the man he was lucky to get that. Then he stood up, turned and looked at the mass of humanity milling around on the sidewalk. Connel scowled. It was a repeat of the night before. Then a Vietnamese man pushed his way through and looked Connel in the eye. "You want to fuck my sister? She's a virgin."

"Sure she is, asshole. Do I look like I just fell off the turnip truck?"

"She's a virgin. Honest to God. I not lie."

"Get away from me."

"Five hundred P," said the man.

Connel put a hand on the man's chest and pushed. The guy stumbled backward and fell. Connel heard him shouting as he walked away, but he didn't care. The man was an asshole.

He moved along the sidewalk, looking at the people around him. The Vietnamese seemed to be subhuman in some respects. At first he couldn't figure out why he felt that and then decided it was because they were all smaller than he was. None of them probably weighed much more than a hundred pounds.

Connel walked on down the street, peering into a couple of bars, listening to the music pumping out of them. There were dancers in some and bar girls in all of them. The dancers sometimes wore bikinis, but more often than not were naked. GIs crowded into the bars, screaming, shouting and waving their money, unable to spend it fast enough. Vietnamese women hung on to the GIs, tricking them into spending their money.

"This is bullshit," said Connel. He stopped on the sidewalk, looked back into the street and realized he just wanted to get out of there. He wanted nothing to do with the Vietnamese. They weren't even worth the effort it took to knock them down.

THE LAST OF THE LITTLE light faded from the jungle. During the day the jungle had been a glowing green hell; now it was as dark as a coal mine. The scant light provided by the moon and stars was absorbed by the jungle. But even they weren't visible now. The storms that had threatened all day had finally arrived. Gerber knew it was raining. He could hear thunder rumbling overhead and the sizzling sound of heavy rain. And once in a while there was a bright flash of lightning. But, strangely enough, the water wasn't hitting the ground. The triple canopy of the jungle absorbed it.

Fetterman crouched near Gerber. "You ready to go, Captain?"

Gerber took a deep breath. "No, but let's do it, anyway."

Fetterman turned and looked at the closest Vietnamese striker. "You'll have to wait quietly. We might not be back until the day after tomorrow."

"We wait here."

"If we need help, we'll call on the survival radio. We'll check in at midnight, six and noon."

"I understand."

Fetterman glanced at Gerber. "If you're ready, sir," he said again.

"Let's do it."

Fetterman stepped off, stopped, then pressed on. Gerber stayed close to him. With the noise from the storm overhead and the lack of light, he couldn't hear the master sergeant and could barely see him. Fetterman was little more than a dark, human-sized smudge moving through the blackness of the jungle.

They didn't make much progress because they had to feel their way along, searching for booby traps, though neither thought they would find any. No American or South Vietnamese forces had penetrated the valley in a long time, and Charlie didn't booby-trap the jungle where the Americans didn't operate.

The trip down the slope was easier than the hike up it. They worked their way through the vines and around the thick trees, then crossed a small stream. When they reached the valley floor, they stopped and Fetterman drew close to Gerber. "I suggest we keep moving north."

"Fine."

"In about ten minutes."

"You tired?"

"No, sir. Just figured that it wouldn't hurt to sit here for a moment."

"Anytime."

Fetterman finally got up. Without a word he started to move deeper into the valley. They worked their way around a huge outcropping of rock and into an area where the undergrowth had been stripped away. Even in the dark they could see that the jungle floor had the appearance of a well-manicured park.

"Looks like the enemy's been here," said Fetterman quietly.

Then, almost as if to prove him right, a shape moved in the distance. Both Gerber and Fetterman froze. Neither of them dropped to the ground. When the man disappeared, Fetterman slipped to the rear. Gerber joined him, and they crouched among the bushes and ferns that marked the edge of the jungle.

"One man isn't a buildup," said Gerber.

"This is obviously some kind of enemy camp."

"Let's stay on the perimeter and see what we can find. We'll have to be careful."

"Yes, sir."

Fetterman slipped off and Gerber followed him. Now they were moving more slowly, watching the jungle to their left and the open area under the canopy to their right. They listened for sounds that the enemy was close, but the noise from the thunderstorm masked any sound the VC might make.

They came to an area studded with low bunkers made of dirt reinforced with teak logs and camouflaged by ferns and vines. Fetterman explored the first one, searching it with his fingertips, using his eyes occasionally. But it was too dark to see much of anything.

Gerber searched the next one, then they both pulled back. The bunkers had been abandoned, but they were in good repair, which meant the VC weren't using them at the moment but that they had checked them sometime in the past few days.

They retreated to the jungle cover again. Gerber stretched out on the wet jungle floor and listened to the sounds of the rain on the triple canopy. Some of the massive leaves would fill slowly with rain, then turn over and dump the water, which would crash through the jungle, sounding like a wild animal running or a soldier who wasn't very smart.

There was motion in front of them, men slipping from one area to another. Once he caught the silhouette of an AK-47, and another man seemed to be wearing a helmet. But there weren't a lot of soldiers. Not the numbers he had expected after what Maxwell had said.

"Maybe later in the night," said Fetterman.

"Maybe not," answered Gerber. "This might be a big base, but there's no one here."

"We need to give them a chance."

Gerber shook his head, even though he knew the master sergeant wouldn't be able to see the gesture. It was all going too easily. Maxwell had given them the approximate location of an enemy buildup, and they had used a map to figure out the most likely area to search.

They had slipped in without seeing a sign of the enemy until they'd gotten down into the valley. He just couldn't believe it.

The sudden burst of gunfire caught them both by surprise. It was behind them. Gerber turned to look, but there was nothing to see, just the fading echoes of a machine gun on full-auto in the distance.

"Top of the ridge?" asked Fetterman.

"Sounded like it, but with the way noise echoes around here, I don't know for sure."

"Means they got behind us."

Gerber got to his knees and turned around, staring into the blackness. A single shot reverberated down the hill, but no muzzle-flash was visible.

Fetterman pulled out his survival radio. He extended the antenna and whispered, "Zulu One, this is Zulu Five." He let go of the button and lifted the radio to his ear, listening to the quiet hiss of the carrier wave.

Firing erupted again. It sounded like an RPD. Then they heard what sounded like AKs. Maybe a dozen of them. And, finally, the return of M-16s on full-auto.

"Nothing on the radio, Captain."

Gerber wiped a hand over his face. "I've seen enough here. Let's get back up the hill."

"Going to take a while. We don't want to get stupid."

"Then we better get going."

"Right."

Fetterman stood and moved to the right. He lifted the radio to his lips and whispered, "Zulu One, this is Five." Still nothing. He collapsed the antenna and put the radio away. "I'm ready."

They moved out, diverting to the west. Fetterman found a trail and they crossed it, afraid of running into an ambush along it. Charlie would have no reason to suspect Americans to come out of the valley, but a good commander, with the resources to cover everything, would cover all possibilities so that he didn't get any unpleasant surprises.

They moved faster now, even though they had to climb upward. Dodging around a huge teak tree, Fetterman stepped up on a boulder and dropped momentarily out of sight on the other side. As he did, more firing came from the top of the ridge. Then there was a detonation that sounded like an American-made grenade. It had a strong, flat bang, unlike the muted pop of the Chicom weapons.

"Our boys are still in it," Gerber said.

Fetterman nodded. He didn't say anything. He just pressed on, heading up the hill.

The firing was coming faster, the individual shots combining into a single, drawn-out detonation. Now they were able to see muted muzzle-flashes, and stray rounds snapped through the canopy overhead.

They reached the top of the ridge and stopped. Through gaps in the vegetation, they could now see the strobing of M-16s and AKs firing on full-auto. Bullets whipped through the jungle. There was a muffled detonation from a Chicom grenade.

Fetterman leaned close. "Our guys there. The enemy over there."

"Get on the radio."

Fetterman extended the antenna of the survival radio and whispered, "Zulu One, this is Five." Still there was no answer. "I think they're busy."

"Okay, we'll have to hope they're smart enough not to open up on us, too. Let's see about getting behind the VC."

"Rifles or grenades?"

"Let's use grenades first. Rifles if we have to."

Fetterman put the radio away and checked his weapon again, knowing full well it was ready.

Gerber pointed to the left where two AKs were firing on full-auto. He held a grenade up so that Fetterman could see it. When the master sergeant nodded, Gerber pulled the pin. He came up on one knee and cocked his arm. There was a burst from one of the AKs, giving him a perfect target. He threw the grenade and let the motion carry him forward, dropping him onto his face.

He closed his eyes just as the grenade exploded. There was a sharp detonation and then a rainstorm of dirt, debris and shrapnel. Gerber came up again, his M-16 at the ready, but the AKs were no longer firing.

Fetterman moved then, slipping back down the slope. Gerber followed him as they worked their way around behind the VC. From the jungle came the sounds of enemy soldiers trying to slip closer to the strikers. There were quiet commands in Vietnamese and the ever-present firing of weapons.

Gerber slipped on the wet ground and fell to one knee. As he did, one of the VC opened fire to the rear. The rounds snapped overhead, cutting through the vegetation and slamming into the tree trunks. He rolled to the right but didn't return fire.

"You hit?" asked Fetterman, his voice low.

"I'm fine. Just fell."

There wasn't a response. Just the sudden sound of something thrown through the jungle. Then there was an explosion, and the firing from the enemy soldier ceased.

Fetterman returned and knelt next to Gerber. "Now what?"

"Let's take out as many as we can from back here."

"Yes, sir."

Gerber got to his feet and moved to the left, following Fetterman. Now they could see shadows moving in the jungle above them. Even with the firing of weapons they could hear orders in Vietnamese. An AK fired a burst, stopped and then another fired.

Gerber watched the enemy soldier pop up, shoot, then drop from sight. He raised his rifle and waited. When the man fired again, Gerber put a burst into him. The VC pitched forward, falling to the jungle floor.

Fetterman fired a burst to his right, and another enemy fell. There was some return fire, but it was wide of the mark. Gerber waited, then put a five-shot burst into the muzzle-flash. As he did, someone shot at him. The rounds were close. He heard them snap by his ears. Fetterman took out that soldier with a single round.

When there was a rattling in the trees, Gerber recognized it immediately. A grenade. He dropped forward and clapped his hands over his ears as the Chicom grenade exploded. It was close enough for him to feel its flash of heat, but the shrapnel was all above him.

A shape appeared in the darkness. Gerber rolled right and fired once, but the VC didn't move or shoot back. Gerber slowly stood and realized he'd just put a burst into a tree stump.

"You okay?" asked Fetterman again.

"Fine."

But now the enemy was beginning to come toward them. First one man, moving slowly, his head down. Gerber stepped behind him and shot him.

Then others began to approach—in pairs and threes, until finally it looked as if the whole unit was withdrawing. Gerber slipped to the rear, put his back against the smooth bark of a teak tree and watched the moving shadows. He lobbed a grenade over the enemy, letting it explode in front of them. Fetterman did the same.

More grenades detonated. There were muzzle-flashes from the AKs and then a single loud shout. The VC panicked then. One man screamed and the others broke cover, racing down the slope. The firing from them tapered and stopped.

Fetterman loomed out of the darkness. "Captain."

"Radio."

Fetterman extracted the radio and pulled out the antenna. "Zulu One, this is Five."

"Go, Five."

"Enemy on the run. Be advised we are close to your location. Coming in."

"Roger."

Fetterman started to collapse the antenna, then stopped. He kept the radio high, close to his ear. He wanted to be able to talk to the strikers if he needed to. To Gerber, he asked, "Are you ready?"

Gerber was on his feet. "Let's do it."

"Coming in," Fetterman said again.

They slipped back in the direction they had come, trying to flank the strikers. If they moved directly toward them, someone might accidentally open fire. But then Gerber saw the first of the strikers, a dark human-sized shape against the blackness of the jungle. He pointed the man out to Fetterman, who nodded once. On the radio, he said, "We've got you in sight."

"Roger."

And then they were back among the strikers. Two on one side and another on the other. "What's the situation here?" Gerber asked.

"Two men wounded," one of the strikers answered. "Two dead. One missing. We get out now?"

"Nope," said Fetterman. "Got to find the missing man."

"He dead," said one of the strikers.

"Then we'll find his body and carry it out," said Gerber. He looked at the striker NCO. "How many VC were out there?"

"*Beaucoup* VC. Maybe a hundred."

Gerber laughed. There probably weren't more than thirty. In the dark it might have seemed like more. "Let's get this organized and then get out of here."

Fetterman tapped a man on the chest. "We'll go look for the missing man."

"I'll look at the wounded and then we'll get ready to return to camp."

"Yes, sir," said Fetterman.

Gerber watched the master sergeant disappear, then turned toward the strikers. He wasn't sure if he'd found Maxwell's answer or not. He just knew it was time to get out, before the VC returned with those hundred men that had been reported.

8

TAN SON NHUT
SAIGON

Connel spent the morning wandering among various offices and buildings, trying to learn how to get out to Tay Ninh. Someone had finally told him about Hotel Three, the heliport near the World's Largest PX. He walked by the store, where an armed MP watched as the men came and went. There was a movie theater, and even that early he could smell popcorn. Connel hadn't been in Vietnam long enough to realize how out of place the PX and the theater were.

The road leading to Hotel Three wasn't marked, but the chain-link fence showed him exactly where the field was. He walked around the perimeter, passed through the gate and entered the terminal. Dropping his duffel bag onto the dirty concrete floor, he leaned forward on the waist-high counter. A young man in jungle pants and an OD green T-shirt was standing with his back to him. The man was using a grease-smeared rag to wipe aircraft numbers from the scheduling board. At the other end of the long, narrow building was the waiting room. It contained broken-down furniture, a couple of tables holding ratty-looking magazines and paperback books, and nearly two dozen soldiers, all waiting for rides out into the boondocks.

Connel finally rapped on the counter, and the man turned. "Help you?"

"Need a ride out to Tay Ninh."

The man looked at Connel's stateside fatigues, the insignia still shiny. He saw the short-cropped hair and white face that had yet to see much of the tropical sun. "Chopper making a run out there about ten. You wanna wait for it?"

"Connel."

"Sir?"

"My name for the manifest. Connel. I'll wait."

"No manifest. I'll just shout out the destination and then you hotfoot it out to the chopper."

"Thanks." Connel picked up his duffel bag and moved into the waiting room. He looked down at a soldier in dirty, torn jungle fatigues. The man hadn't shaved in a couple of days and was now lying on the floor, sleeping, oblivious to everything around him. Connel was tempted to kick him awake and point out that he was an American soldier, that there was an image to maintain. But he decided against it. The man was probably a draftee who didn't care about the Army, serving his country or anything else that was important.

Connel didn't like the look of the battered couch or any of the chairs scattered around. He dropped his duffel bag and sat on the end of it, turning so that he could look out onto the airfield.

Helicopters landed and took off periodically. Some parked and shut down. Pilots and crewmen came into the terminal, some announcing that they had room for anyone going to Cu Chi or Trang Bang or Phu Loi. They announced towns that Connel had never heard of and places that he knew from the news reports back in the World. Finally the clerk leaned on his counter and yelled, "Chopper to Tay Ninh's here. It's the one with the old knight's shield on the front."

Connel stood up and shouldered his duffel bag. He stepped to the door and saw the helicopter the clerk had told him about. It sat there, facing him, its rotors whirling rapidly, its engine roaring. Through the windshield, he could see the two pilots. Behind them were the gunners. Both machine guns were pointed down, but there was linked ammo from boxes up into the weapons. As he approached, he yelled at one of the men in the back, "This going to Tay Ninh?"

"Yeah."

Connel tossed his duffel bag up into the cargo compartment and kicked it up next to the pilots' seats. He dropped onto the troop seat and waited.

"Sir," said the crew chief, "would you mind buckling your seat belt?"

"Christ," said Connel. He searched, found the ends and buckled it.

A moment later the chopper came up to a hover. It turned one way and then another, finally lifting up and out. Connel watched the airfield slip away and then saw the heart of Saigon off to his left. Out to the right was the deep green of the countryside. Connel was surprised by that. There didn't seem to be a transition from city to country. Saigon ended abruptly, as if someone had designated an edge to the city. A ribbon of road headed off to the northwest and they seemed to follow it.

The countryside was pretty—deep greens broken only by small villages and large American bases. He looked down at a hamlet filled with mud hootches with tin roofs.

Palm trees shaded it. The road, filled with military vehicles, scooters and oxcarts, wound through it.

They turned away from the road and crossed a forest. Connel had expected to see nothing but triple-canopy jungle, but this was a scraggly forest of short, twisted trees and tall grass. A circular camp was set in the center of the forest, its huge howitzers surrounded by bright green sandbags. The ground around the camp was nearly bare, the earth a deep red.

There was a river off to the north, looping back and forth and sparkling in the morning sun. He saw a forest of green trees that seemed to be lined up like soldiers in formation. That had to be a rubber plantation. In the center of it was a camp, and as they flew past, he saw a swimming pool surrounded by a dozen buildings.

"Dau Tieng!" yelled the crew chief above the noise of the turbine. "Rubber trees belong to the French. Plantation headquarters belongs to us."

Almost as soon as they were beyond that, they were between a huge black mountain, which Connel learned was Nui Ba Den, and the city of Tay Ninh—a real city with tree-lined streets, a huge temple filled with gold and a downtown area of sizable buildings.

They skirted the edge of the city, keeping to the northern side. Connel studied the slopes of Nui Ba Den. It had little vegetation and steep sides. At the summit an American camp bristled with radio antennae.

Next they approached a huge American camp that was nearly as large as Tay Ninh. It was surrounded by a barbed wire perimeter and a line of bunkers. When he saw it, Connel thought of the former Vietcong soldier scampering through the wire without effort. He wondered if the men inside the camp below knew of the ability, or more importantly, if they cared. The VC might be able to sneak through the wire, but once they'd done that, the Americans would kill them quickly. Connel was sure of that.

They entered the traffic pattern and landed a moment later, hovering near a tower before they touched down. The other passengers jumped out. Connel retrieved his duffel bag and climbed out, too. As soon as he was standing on the pad, the chopper lifted, turned and vanished. It was suddenly silent around him. He glanced at the airfield, but there were no aircraft to be seen.

A sergeant approached and said, "If you're Twenty-fifth, I can give you a ride."

Connel shouldered his bag. "Thanks, Sergeant."

They took the jeep to brigade headquarters. The road was muddy from the rain the night before. Both sides were choked with weeds, though someone had poured oil over most of the vegetation in a vain attempt to keep it from serving as a hatching ground for mosquitoes.

Brigade headquarters was a single-story hootch that looked just like all the other plywood-and-tin structures in the camp. Connel took his duffel bag from the rear of the jeep and shouldered it. Waving at the sergeant, he said, "Thanks for the lift, Sarge."

"No problem, Lieutenant."

Connel entered the building and dropped his duffel bag near the door, out of the way. Turning, he spotted a clerk sitting behind a desk. He had blond, longish hair and a feeble attempt at a mustache. He could have been the twin of the clerk in the terminal at Hotel Three.

"Colonel in?" asked Connel.

"Minute." The man didn't look up.

The colonel came through a door that had been closed. He was stout, short and had black hair. His starched fatigues looked as if he'd put them on only minutes earlier. He carried a folder in one hand and was reading a paper in the other.

"Dickens," he said, then looked up. "Who are you?" he asked Connel.

"New man, sir. Just assigned," said the clerk.

The colonel stared at the stateside fatigues and the bright insignia and growled, "Shit, just what I need." He waved a folder at the clerk. "Didn't what's his name, Suttin, say he needed some help?"

The clerk shrugged.

"You got your issue yet?" asked the colonel.

"No, sir," said Connel. "I just got here about a minute ago."

"Shit." He looked at the clerk. "Get this guy his issue and then put him on a chopper out to, ah, shit, what's his name? At Bang Ron?"

"Lieutenant Suttin?"

"Yeah." The colonel turned back to Connel. "Get your issue and then head out to Bang Ron. Report to Lieutenant Suttin."

"Don't I need to sign in here?"

"Fuck it. Suttin will take care of it. Get your issue, your weapon and get the fuck out there."

"But I'm—"

"Pissing me off is what you're doing. Get with the program and get out of here."

"Yes, sir," said Connel. It was the only thing he could say.

The colonel tossed the file onto the desk in front of the clerk and said, "See that Sergeant Robinson gets that and that he reports back to me by 1500 hours. Today. Any excuses and I'll have his ass humping the boondocks by nightfall."

"Yes, sir."

The colonel disappeared into his office. As soon as the door closed, Connel said, "Give me a few clues."

"Supply is out the door, down the street and then back away from the road. Long, low building painted white. Sergeant Schad is the man to see. He'll get you everything you need, including your weapons and ammo."

"And then?"

The clerk took a deep breath. "Chopper out to Bang Ron."

"Are there regular flights?"

"No, sir. I'll have to arrange something."

Connel shrugged. "Okay if I leave my duffel bag here?"

"No one'll steal it if that's what you mean."

"Thanks."

"Sir. The old man's having a bad day. Hell, a bad week. He's usually not that abrupt."

"Sure." Connel turned, but then hesitated. "What's this Bang Ron like?"

"Small camp, but it's not that bad. You'll see. And there aren't any colonels there."

"That's something."

Connel left headquarters, walked down the road and spotted the supply building. He stepped up on a boardwalk made of two-by-twelves, entered through double doors and stopped at a waist-high counter. From the rear he could hear the roar of a fan. Everyone and his brother had a fan in Vietnam. Everyone.

"Sergeant Schad?" he called out.

A giant black man suddenly appeared. He had a bullet-shaped head nearly devoid of hair, and no obvious neck. His hands could have been catchers' mitts. Connel was sure he'd never seen another human of such gigantic proportions. "You want?" the behemoth grunted.

"Need my issue, Sergeant. Basic issue and weapon." Connel was hard-pressed not to say, "sir."

"They didn't get you this stuff down in Saigon?"

"No... nope. Didn't get shit."

Schad grinned and slammed a fistful of papers on the counter. "You fill out these and we'll get you everything you need."

Connel took the forms, picked up a government pen chained to the desk and began to write. As he did, two supply clerks started carrying out everything Connel could possibly want to go to war. There was a mess kit, entrenching tool, tent stakes, shelter half and poncho. They brought out a pistol belt and rucksack. They gave him a combat knife and boots. There were uniforms and underwear, socks and OD-colored towels. They brought him a couple of laundry bags and began stuffing all of the other equipment and uniforms into them.

That finished, Schad appeared with an M-16 and a bandolier of ammo for it. He wrote down the number from the weapon on one of the forms and then set it on the counter. Another of the clerks appeared with a .45-caliber pistol and set it down. He put a holster next to it. In typical Army fashion, the holster was for a .38.

"Sign here and here," said Schad.

Connel took the pen and did as he was told.

Schad took the forms, then said, "Everything here except the weapons is expendable. I don't expect to see any of it back. Hell, I don't want to see any of it ever again. You lose the weapon, there'll be an investigation. You lose it in a combat situation and it's no sweat. You lose it by being stupid, you have to pay for it. Questions?"

"I can take all this home."

"Except for the weapon, yes, sir. If you want to. But who'd want to haul an entrenching tool home? They're just fucked-up little shovels. Get a better one at a hardware store for a couple of bucks."

"Didn't say I wanted to, Sergeant. Just asked if I could if I did want to."

"Then, yes, sir, you can take it home."

Connel stuffed the pistol and holster into one of the laundry bags. Shouldering the bandolier and M-16, he picked up the laundry bags and was surprised at how heavy they were. Then he walked out the door and back to headquarters.

As he stepped in the doorway, Dickens, the clerk, said, "Glad you're here, sir. Got a chopper ride for you. Have to get over to the heliport right now, though."

"How about a lift to the pad?"

The clerk looked at the closed door to the colonel's office and then nodded. "Come on."

Together they carried his gear out to a jeep and loaded it in the back. The clerk drove and Connel held on as they roared along the dirty roads. They reached the heliport a few minutes later, driving up to the only helicopter sitting there. While the clerk confirmed that it was the right aircraft, Connel unloaded his gear.

"That's them, sir," Dickens told him.

Connel stuck out a hand. "Thanks."

"If I were you, Lieutenant, I'd come back next week and report to the colonel proper. He should be in a better mood by then and I think he'd appreciate it."

"Sure."

Connel then loaded his gear into the rear of the chopper and climbed aboard. A moment later they took off. Connel had been at Tay Ninh for almost a whole hour.

It was hard to believe that so much had happened in so little time.

As he settled down on the troop seat, they climbed out to the north. He realized that helicopters were used in Vietnam the same way trucks and buses were used in the World. The South Vietnamese road system wasn't very good and there was always a real possibility of ambush. Helicopters didn't need roads, didn't need much in the way of a landing zone, and weren't as prone to ambush as ground vehicles.

He leaned back against the soundproofing. The engine noise had increased, the blades were popping and the wind was whipping past, making conversation impossible. He glanced right and left. The door gunners were sitting behind their weapons, ignoring everything.

Connel did notice a change in the landscape below him. Around Saigon the jungle had been thin, what little there was. Open ground stretched far to the south and there was a scraggly forest to the west until it shifted to jungle. But north of Tay Ninh it was all jungle. There were no breaks for rice paddies or farms except along the banks of the larger rivers. The jungle spread out in front of them in a long, almost unbroken mass.

Finally he noticed a break in the canopy in front of them. As they approached, the camp began to take on shape. First it was an oval in the jungle, then it began to change until he could see buildings, bunkers and a perimeter.

There was a tap on his shoulder and the door gunner leaned around from his well. "There it is."

Connel nodded. As he watched, a cloud of green smoke appeared, growing rapidly. The chopper began a long descent toward the camp. They circled it once, then fell out of the sky, landing with the nose of the aircraft over the billowing smoke grenade.

As the skids touched the ground at the end of the runway, close to the gate, the crew chief was up and moving. He grabbed one of the equipment bags and dropped it onto the red dirt of the runway. Connel climbed out and turned, grabbing his duffel bag to drag it out of the cargo compartment. The crew chief slid the other equipment bag at him, and as Connel grabbed it, the chopper rose. Before Connel could take two steps, it was up and away. The rotor wash tore at the surface of the runway, creating a cloud of dense red dust. Connel turned his back and closed his eyes. The sound of the turbine changed slightly, then began to fade into the distance as the cloud of dust thinned rapidly.

"Welcome to Bang Ron," said a voice.

Connel opened his eyes and saw a man standing there. "I'm Lieutenant Suttin." He held out his hand.

"Connel." He shook hands with the other officer, who had no weapon at all. He stood there in sweat-stained jungle fatigues, looking as if he were on a base in the World.

"Let me give you a hand with your gear and we'll get off this exposed strip." He picked up one of the laundry bags and slung it over his shoulder. "You don't know how happy I am that you've joined us."

Connel looked at the camp and thought about the pictures he'd seen of the squalor in Third World countries—people living in poverty, the shelter they found little more than packing crates or mud huts. Compared to what he was seeing now, that looked almost luxurious. "How many men are here?" he asked.

Suttin started toward the gate. He walked slowly, letting Connel catch up to him. "We've got twenty-three

Americans. Twenty-five if you count the two Green Berets who are working with us at the moment. And we've got a 147 South Vietnamese strikers.''

"Where do they live? The Vietnamese."

"In the camp with us. Why? You got something against the Vietnamese?"

"No," said Connel. "Just curious."

They entered the camp and headed across it to a small hootch. Suttin dropped the equipment near the door. "These are my quarters. There's an extra cot in there that you can have. We've got a few luxuries the enlisted men don't have, but we'll have to share the room."

"I don't mind," said Connel.

"I've got a dozen things to do, and we've got a patrol coming in that got zapped. You get settled here."

Connel nodded. He glanced at the tiny hootch. There was a wall of sandbags around it that had obviously seen better days. "Take many mortar shells?"

"Once or twice a week." Suttin grinned. "Welcome to Bang Ron."

9

JUNGLE NORTH OF
BANG RON

With the first light, Gerber and Fetterman made plans
to get the hell out of there. The wounded men hadn't
been badly hurt, and no one was in danger of dying. The
dead had been located and the bodies wrapped in poncho liners.

After the battle, they had moved from the site, afraid
that the enemy would try to sneak back in to kill them.
They had moved three hundred yards to the right and
had settled in, Gerber at one end of the line and Fetterman at the other. They stayed in touch by survival radio.

But the night had passed quietly, with only the sounds
of the animals to keep them awake. The rain that had
been falling above them drifted away, and the weather
changed slightly, becoming a little cooler and damper.
Gerber, resting on one knee so that he wouldn't fall
asleep, had studied the jungle around him, certain that
he was surrounded by enemy soldiers. There were human shapes barely visible in the charcoal gray, but the
shapes never seemed to move, and Gerber knew they
were bushes, trees and ferns playing tricks on him.

At dawn they pulled together, forming a loose circle. Half of the men ate breakfast while the other half guarded. Then positions were reversed. Gerber sat with his back to a log and ate his scrambled eggs cold. The food was a pressed, yellow mess masquerading as scrambled eggs, and cardboard had more taste.

Fetterman crouched near Gerber and glanced into the OD-colored can at the scrambled eggs. "How can you eat that shit cold?"

"Because I'm hungry and it's the only thing available right now."

Fetterman shook his head.

"It's got to be better than the rations you had during World War II."

"Maybe and maybe not," said Fetterman. "I wouldn't eat them, either."

Gerber dropped the white spoon into the can and set it aside. "What's on your mind?"

"Still got that man missing. Now that it's light, I'd like to go find him."

Gerber pulled at the camouflage cover on his watch and checked the time. "An hour do it?"

"Should be more than enough time."

"Okay, but remember, we've got wounded. We need to get them into the camp."

"Can't leave the man," said Fetterman.

"I know," said Gerber. "I'll wait for a while, then head back. You'll have to catch up to us, but don't get too far behind."

"I understand, sir."

"We'll take it slow until you catch up."

"Yes, sir." Fetterman moved off, tapped one man on the shoulder and then another. They slipped to the center of the tiny perimeter, where Fetterman briefed them quickly.

As he did, Gerber stood up and moved where the wounded lay. One man was asleep and the other awake. Both wounds were little more than scratches, but in the jungle a scratch could prove fatal. Too many germs around. Infection was the biggest danger.

Gerber took a deep breath and wished they could get out immediately. He watched Fetterman slip through the perimeter and out into the jungle.

FETTERMAN DIDN'T HESITATE. He walked toward the scene of the battle. The missing man had probably been killed during the fighting. In the dark they hadn't been able to locate the body. Now, in the light, he hoped to find it.

He moved slowly, listening for sounds that the VC had returned. They always dragged off their dead. They didn't want the Americans to know how many soldiers they lost. If the Americans couldn't count the body, then the man wasn't really dead. It was the other side of the stupid game played by the brass hats in Saigon and Washington.

He stepped over a log, halted and fell to one knee. Listening, he stood up, his weapon at the ready. A bird cried out, the call echoing through the jungle. It was answered by another, then another.

One of the strikers came up beside Fetterman and held up a hand. The man froze. Fetterman pointed to the left, and the striker moved in that direction. He stepped carefully, easing his weight onto each foot so that he didn't snap a twig or depress a pressure plate.

Fetterman glanced right and left. The leaves of a bush had been shredded by the firefight during the night. The material stripped from the plants covered the jungle floor like light green frost.

Slipping forward cautiously, Fetterman spotted a pool of blood. The surface was dark and crusted over. Huge flies, their bodies fluorescent blue or green, were moving around the edges of it. Their buzzing was loud and insistent.

He found a body, one of the enemy killed by a grenade. The front of his black pajamas were ripped and his blood had formed in a pool around his head, as if he were wearing a dark, gory halo. Flies covered the body in a single, wriggling mass so that it looked as if the skin were shifting and surging.

Fetterman picked up the AK the man had dropped. Even with the moisture it had picked up lying on the jungle floor, it was in mint condition, a perfect souvenir. The Saigon armchair commandos would pay a premium for the weapon. Or the perfect trading material for something you couldn't get through channels. Fetterman slung it and continued forward.

Now he noticed the morning sounds. Monkeys scampered through the trees, chattering. Birds flapped their wings. Lizards rustled in the undergrowth. And rats were beginning to find the bodies. He could see a large brown one right in front of him. It rocked back on its hind feet, ready to defend its meal. But then the rat realized the master sergeant was too big, so it whirled and disappeared.

Fetterman and the strikers worked their way along the line they had defended the night before. There was more blood. Another body and another weapon, but this one had been damaged by shrapnel. The stock was shattered but the breech, trigger housing and barrel seemed intact. A new stock would make it worth money in Saigon. Fetterman added it to his collection.

Fetterman looked at the dead man. He lay facedown but there was no sign of a wound or blood. Fetterman rolled him over, using the toe of his boot. It looked as if the enemy had been gutted. His intestines, stomach, liver and heart lay on the ground. The man had fallen on his internal organs.

"Here," said one of the strikers suddenly. "Here."

Fetterman glanced at him, then moved over. They had found the missing striker. There was a single bullet hole in the side of the man's head. The striker had probably died instantly.

"Wrap up the body and let's get out of here," ordered Fetterman.

The two strikers did as they were told. They shook out a poncho liner and wrapped the body in it. One of the strikers handed his rifle to the other, then lifted the dead man, throwing him over his shoulder in a fireman's carry.

Fetterman hesitated for a moment, wondering if he should try to get a good body count. Maxwell would want one. Then he grinned and figured that if Maxwell needed one that badly, he could fly out and get it himself. "Go," he told the strikers.

Before leaving himself, he listened to the jungle, but there was nothing to suggest that the enemy was close. He surveyed his surroundings carefully. The enemy was there all right. He didn't know how many of them or exactly where, but he suspected they had honeycombed the floor of the valley with tunnels and bunkers. It would take an American division to root them out, and then the enemy might simply vanish, slipping into the jungle while the Americans worked their way closer.

Following the two Vietnamese strikers, Fetterman protected the rear, ever vigilant for signs of the enemy. He watched the strikers force their way through the jungle, leaving a noticeable trail. But he didn't care. He knew they'd be out of the field by noon, long before Charlie could get into position to ambush them.

GERBER GOT THE MEN READY, decided that he would take the point and let the senior striker NCO have the responsibility for the rear guard. He waited for Fetterman, but when the hour was up, he started off.

They didn't hurry. They worked through the jungle, moving down the slope they had climbed the day before. In the distance they could hear choppers and artillery, and once a flight of fighters. Sunlight filtered through the occasional gap in the triple canopy, and the jungle began to feel like a steam bath.

He kept the pace slow, stopping frequently, always listening for Fetterman on the survival radio. Finally the radio crackled to life. "Zulu Six, this is Zulu Five."

"Go, Five."

"We're about a hundred yards behind you."

"Roger. Were you successful?"

"Roger. We located the package, but it was damaged. Badly damaged."

"Understand. No need for Medevac?"

"That's a negative."

"Roger." Gerber held up a hand and stopped the patrol. He spread them out, warning them that Fetterman and the others would be coming in. No one was to fire unless Gerber gave them permission to do so.

The strikers appeared a moment later. They came toward the center of the perimeter and dropped the corpse onto the ground. None of the other strikers moved.

They maintained their positions just as they had been ordered to do.

Gerber met Fetterman at the edge. "See anything significant?"

"No, sir. A few bodies, but nothing more." He unslung the captured AK and showed it to the captain.

"I don't like this," said Gerber. "They broke contact but didn't try to recover the dead or weapons."

"Maybe they're planning to return in the morning with a large force. Figured to overwhelm us then."

"Except they haven't done that," said Gerber.

"No, sir."

"I think we'd better get on our horses and get out of here while we can."

"Yes, sir."

"You want to take point?"

"No, sir. You're doing a fine job of leading the unit. I'd like to hang back."

"I'm not going to stop until we're in sight of the camp. About two, three hours."

"That's a hell of a walk."

"Nothing these guys can't do. Besides, it's either downhill or level. We'll be in by noon."

"I'll keep you advised of the situation back here," said Fetterman.

"You do that."

Gerber moved back to the front of the perimeter. He hesitated there, took a drink from his canteen and wiped the sweat from his face. Around him was nothing but jungle. There was only a little light. It looked like dusk, but he knew it was the middle of the morning. Sunlight just didn't penetrate some sections of the jungle.

Finished with his canteen, he capped it and put it back into its holder. Then, wiping his lips, he lifted a hand and told the strikers to move out. They filed in behind him, and Gerber started off again. He kept the pace slow, making it easier on the men, avoiding the thickest of the undergrowth.

They came to a stream and Gerber plunged into it. On the other side, he halted and waited. When most of the strikers were across, he started off again, walking around a clump of bamboo and then around a huge teak tree. There were initials carved in the trunk, telling him that someone had been there in 1964.

Finally, up ahead, he saw the jungle beginning to brighten. It was the edge of the killing zone around the camp. He slowed again, giving the men a chance to catch up. When he reached the very edge of the killing zone, he stopped.

Using his binoculars, he checked the camp. Beyond the bunkers, barely visible, he could see strikers working. They were building new structures and sandbagging them. The runway was deserted, as was the fire control tower.

Gerber moved over to the RTO and used the PRC-25. With the handset clamped to his ear, he said, "Headhunter Base, this is Zulu Six."

There was a moment of silence, then, "This is Headhunter Base. Go, Six."

"We're ready to come in."

"Can you throw smoke?"

"Roger, smoke." Gerber snapped his fingers at one of the strikers.

The man moved to the very edge of the jungle and tossed a smoke grenade into the killing zone. A moment later the man on the radio said, "ID purple."

"Roger, purple."

"Come on in."

"Roger. Be advised we have wounded. Have the medic standing by. No wounds are serious."

"Roger, that. Anything else?"

"That's a negative."

"Roger."

Gerber tossed the handset back to the RTO and stood up. He checked behind him, making sure everyone was in place and set to move. At the far end of the line, barely visible through the vegetation, stood Fetterman. He held his weapon in both hands and was studying the killing field in front of them. He was ready.

Gerber turned and stepped into the zone, avoiding the stinking cloud of purple smoke that was beginning to drift off to the right. As they reached the runway, a truck burst from the camp. It roared up and stopped suddenly, its wheels locking so that it slid on the dirt surface, kicking up a cloud of red dust. The morning sun had dried most of the rain from the night before, and the few remaining puddles looked like pools of diluted blood.

"The wounded?" said the driver, leaning out the window, as if he were a New York hack.

Gerber hooked a thumb over his shoulder, pointing to the rear. The two wounded men came forward slowly and climbed into the rear. The men carrying the bodies also appeared. A striker opened the tailgate and helped them as they pushed the bodies onto the bed. When the truck was loaded, it spun around, throwing up a rooster tail of dirt as it rocketed toward the gate.

Gerber reached the edge of the runway, and as he did, Suttin appeared at the gate. He stood there for a moment, then walked forward, almost casually. "What happened?"

"Ran into the VC last night."

"Bad?"

Gerber shrugged. "I think it was worse for them. We don't have a good body count, but they lost fifteen, maybe twenty killed."

Suttin moved in closer. "Your friend Maxwell has been on the radio every hour on the hour. Wants to talk to you as soon as possible."

"We didn't learn anything that important for him," said Gerber.

The whole patrol had crossed the runway and was beginning to straggle toward the gate. They looked tired, and if they followed their whims, they'd want to eat and sleep. Gerber nodded to Fetterman. "Get a weapons check made and then get everyone a good lunch."

"Yes, sir."

"I'll check on the wounded." Gerber looked at Suttin. "We might need to evac them."

"You keep getting my men sent off the base," said Suttin quietly.

Gerber shot him a glance, then realized Suttin was kidding. The joke was fairly lame.

"What about Maxwell?" asked Fetterman.

"We still don't have anything concrete for him. Just some indications."

"That mean another patrol in there?"

Gerber watched as the last of the strikers entered the camp. He moved closer to Fetterman and Suttin. "I think we better put two, three patrols in and have them look around. There are indications that Charlie's there, but he's being careful. I want to know why."

"What about the families?" asked Suttin.

Gerber rubbed his face. "You got room for them here inside the perimeter?"

"Be crowded. Some of the men would end up sleeping in the open, and we'll have trouble feeding everyone, but I think we can manage it."

"I know how the Vietnamese think," said Gerber. "If they know their families are safe, or at the very least with them, then they'll do a better job for us. I think it's time to bring them in."

"Yes, sir," said Suttin.

"Tony, I'm going to ride in with the wounded, then head down to talk with Maxwell and see what he has on his mind that's so important. You'd better catch some sleep, then take out a patrol tonight. Not too far. Just out to see if the enemy's patrolling at all. An easy, quiet sweep designed to find the enemy."

"Yes, sir."

Gerber frowned. "You know, there's something I'm missing here, but I'm damned if I can think of it."

"Probably think of it later," said Fetterman.

"Yeah. I hope so. I sure as hell hope so."

10

BANG RON

Suttin pointed across the table. "Sergeant Fetterman, this is Lieutenant Connel. He arrived this morning. Fresh from the World."

Fetterman held out a hand. "Nice to meet you, Lieutenant."

Connel nodded. "You're not assigned here permanently?"

"No, sir. I work with Special Forces in Saigon. Captain Gerber and I have been doing some work for MACV Headquarters."

Suttin sat down. "Sergeant Fetterman, or rather Captain Gerber, suggested that we need to run a few more patrols out into the field." He turned his attention to Connel. "Sergeant Fetterman will be taking one out about dusk and I think you'd learn a lot by accompanying him."

"Sure," said Connel. "Who'll be in charge?"

Suttin looked at Fetterman, then back at the lieutenant. "Ah, given the fact you've been here only a day and in-country a week, I think Sergeant Fetterman should be in charge."

"He's a sergeant."

"Sir," said Fetterman, "I think we're getting off the subject. If Lieutenant Connel feels he should be in command, then appoint him." Looking at Connel, Fetterman added, "But I would hope, sir, that you'd be clever enough to realize that since I'm on my second tour I have things to teach you."

Connel smiled, but it was a thin smile. He nodded. "Of course, Sergeant."

"If a situation develops with us in contact," continued Fetterman, "I hope the lieutenant will realize that I've been in contact with the enemy before."

"I expect advice," said Connel.

Suttin shook his head. "I've heard stories from the old days where American advisers, because they didn't command, had trouble getting the men to do what had to be done...."

Fetterman coughed. "I'm sure Lieutenant Connel realizes that a soldier who has fought in three different wars, regardless of rank, knows the score."

"Of course," said Connel.

"Then that's settled," said Suttin. "Sergeant Fetterman will show you the ropes of patrolling in the jungle. Listen to him and learn."

Connel laughed. "I thought we had a week of orientation before we ended up in the field."

"And you would have," said Suttin, "except that I'm shorthanded and there's no way to teach you what you have to know except to throw you out into the field."

"I think we have that settled," said Connel. "Now what are we supposed to learn out there?"

Fetterman got to his feet. "We want to see what the enemy response is. We know they're out there, but we don't know their numbers or what they've got on their minds. All we know is that something funny is going on.''

GERBER RODE the Medevac chopper to Tay Ninh and then caught another to Saigon. He landed at Hotel Three and walked over to the MACV-SOG building, where he got a jeep from one of the sergeants on the radio watch.

He drove out the front gate and was going to head directly over to MACV Headquarters but decided a shower and change of clothes couldn't hurt. He stopped near his hotel, locked the jeep and walked to the front door. Entering the lobby, he crossed to the check-in desk and retrieved his key, then headed for the elevator. He rode up alone, walked down the hall and entered his room, hoping Robin might still be there, but she wasn't.

Disappointed, he sat down on the bed and realized the room felt like a stale inferno. Leaning forward, he turned the air conditioner on. A moment later the air was cooler, and Gerber leaned back to enjoy it for a few minutes.

Taking off his boots, he kicked them aside. Then stripped, headed for the bathroom and started the water. A hot bath should make him feel human again. He climbed into the tub and turned slowly, washing the grime and sweat from his body. When he was finished, he turned off the water and stepped out of the tub. He toweled himself, dropped the towel onto the floor and walked back into the other room.

Taking a deep breath, he sat down on the bed. As he did, he realized how tired he was. Too much had been crammed into the past few days, with nothing to really show for it except a couple of dead men.

He lay back, his hands under his head, and stared up at the ceiling for a moment. The overhead fan turned slowly, hypnotically. He watched it until the blades blurred and he couldn't focus on them. Soon he was fast asleep.

THE PATROL FORMED near the gate, as usual, each man with his weapon, rucksack and equipment. As he'd done before, Fetterman checked each man carefully, making sure nothing had been thrown away. Satisfied, he returned to Connel, who stood to one side, watching.

"Have to check them closely, huh?" the lieutenant asked.

"No, sir," said Fetterman. "They expect a good inspection, so I provide them with one."

"But they'd throw shit away if you didn't keep on them, right?"

"Not these men. They've been well trained. They're good soldiers."

"If they're so good," asked Connel, "how come they can't beat the VC?"

"These guys could. I'd match them against any unit the VC could field. Or the North Vietnamese, for that matter."

"Sure," said Connel, shaking his head in disgust.

"You got a problem?" asked Fetterman.

"It's these damn Vietnamese. Dumb fucks can't do a thing for themselves. We have to do it all for them."

Fetterman wasn't sure what to say to that. Anything he said would be ignored by Connel. The man wasn't prepared to believe anything good about the Vietnamese. "You sure you want to go out on this?"

"Hell, no," said Connel. "Do you?"

Fetterman had to grin. The man was right about that. He'd much rather be in Saigon, eating a big dinner, or better yet, back in the World.

"Are you ready, sir?" asked Fetterman.

"Anytime."

Fetterman turned to the strikers and pointed at one man, waving him out. The man exited through the gate and walked across the runway into the grassy field that led to the jungle. Fetterman watched as the patrol began to filter out. As the last of the Vietnamese took off, Fetterman joined them, with Connel right behind him.

They worked their way across the field and reached the jungle thirty minutes later. Fanning out, they entered the trees, then halted. Connel dropped to the ground. His face was bathed in sweat and his uniform was soaked. He was breathing hard and sounded as if he'd run into the jungle rather than walked. "Christ!" he gasped.

"Lot harder than it looks," Fetterman commented.

"I didn't know I was that out of shape," Connel said, shaking his head in disgust.

"Tropics will do that to you."

They sat there for a few minutes, and Connel's breathing slowed. He lifted a hand and wiped the sweat from his face. Finally he said, "I'm ready."

GERBER WOKE WITH A START. His whole body had gone suddenly rigid and he had nearly leaped from the bed. For an instant he wasn't sure where he was. All he knew was that his weapon wasn't near his hand and that it was unusually cold. Then the hum of the air conditioner and the soft sounds from the street drifted up to him.

He sat up and shifted around, his feet on the floor. Looking at the darkened room, he knew that he shouldn't have fallen asleep. That was the mark of an amateur. Even if it was an accident, it wasn't right, not with Fetterman still out in the field.

Gerber got up and put on a clean uniform, then tucked his Browning into the waistband of his trousers so that it was hidden under his jungle jacket. Finally, after glancing around the room once, he headed for the door.

Downstairs in the lobby he stopped and surveyed the crowd. No one seemed concerned about the war. Every man in the lobby was preoccupied with other matters, particularly sex.

Outside, where it was still hot even though the sun was long gone, Gerber walked to his jeep. He unlocked it, climbed in and fired up the engine. When there was a break in the traffic, he pulled out and drove toward the MACV compound, which never closed down. After five o'clock the war was left to the lower-ranking people, the majors, captains and sergeants. But Maxwell rarely left the building, hiding out in his office most of the time. Gerber parked the jeep and walked up to the building. The guards stationed around the outside didn't bother him; he was obviously an American.

The interior of MACV Headquarters wasn't the beehive of activity it was during the day, but it was still busy. Gerber headed down the basement stairs, signed in at the gate after learning that Maxwell was still in his office, then walked down to it and knocked on the door.

"I thought you were in the field," Maxwell said when he opened the door.

"I was."

Maxwell stepped back and let Gerber enter. Then he closed the door and returned to his desk. "I'm pretty busy," he said grumpily.

Gerber dropped into the visitor's chair. "I'm not sure I care all that much."

"What did you want?"

"I'd like to know what you think you know about the area around Bang Ron."

Maxwell picked up a file folder, made a production about reading something in it, then dropped it back on the pile on his desk. "Bang Ron?"

"Come on, Jerry, don't play your spook games with me. You've put us out into the field to look for something."

"And what did you find?"

"We didn't see much traffic on the Trail, as you know. But we've run into the VC every time we've ventured out north of Bang Ron. So what in hell's going on?"

"Significant contact?"

"No. Platoon-sized contact, but with the VC making quick withdrawals. Bodies were left on the field, along with weapons, which is unusual for Charlie."

"What does that tell you?" asked Maxwell.

"First, let me ask you a question," said Gerber. "What did those prisoners I brought in tell you?"

Maxwell shrugged. "Nothing significant. Just that they had walked down the Trail from their homes in North Vietnam and that they were told they would be in on the destruction of South Vietnam."

"Nothing about the tactical situation?"

"Nothing at all."

Gerber shrugged. "Well, I suppose privates in our Army aren't that well informed, either."

"So," said Maxwell, "now it's your turn. You mentioned the tactics of the VC in the past few days. What about it?"

"Charlie's covering for something. When he starts breaking contact when he's got the advantage, and when he leaves his dead on the field, he's trying to send a message. He's trying to tell us he has almost no men around.

He doesn't have the numbers to recover the dead. He breaks contact because he thinks he's outnumbered.''

"But you don't think that?"

"Anytime the enemy changes their tactics, then I get suspicious, because it usually means they're covering for something else, something bigger."

"You see anything to suggest that?" asked Maxwell.

Gerber took a deep breath and twisted around so that he was leaning on the side of Maxwell's desk. "We did a quick patrol of that area you were interested in. We saw a few men running around in the jungle and found an area that seemed to be a huge abandoned base, then we ran into the enemy full force."

"Which tells you?"

"Shit, Maxwell, I don't have to spell it out, do I? Charlie's building a large force in that valley, but he's trying to be careful. He doesn't want us to explore the valley too carefully, not until he's ready."

"Your recommendation?"

Now Gerber grinned broadly. "Put the Air Force on it and have them bomb the hell out of the jungle."

"But we've found that high-altitude bombings of the jungle aren't effective."

"But if there are bombs falling all around, Charlie's going to have to move his base of operations, or he's going to get killed. If he moves, then he's exposed and we can get at him. Also, if he moves to avoid bombs, he can't organize an attack anywhere else."

Maxwell laughed. "I think you've done your job. I'll meet with the general and tell him. We'll get the bombing missions laid on."

"Let us know. Suttin and Fetterman are still running patrols into that area."

"You'll be advised." Maxwell picked up a folder to indicate the meeting was over, then he looked at Gerber. "What are you going to do tonight?"

Gerber shrugged. "I was planning to find a chopper and get back out to Bang Ron. Now I guess I'll see if I can find Robin, have a good dinner and get some sleep. I'll head back tomorrow."

"Have Suttin pull in his patrols when you get there."

Gerber could take a hint. "Certainly."

THEY REACHED THE TOP of the ridge line after a couple of hours of walking. The pointman kept the pace steady, taking frequent breaks in case the enemy was following them. But even so, they made good time.

Fetterman, in the rear with Connel, was surprised by the new guy. He was good in the jungle. He knew how to move through it without disturbing the ground or leaving any signs. He didn't make the kind of noise a new guy usually did. And he was alert. Fetterman noticed that he held his weapon in both hands, ready to fire it, and he kept his head moving, searching the ground, the jungle, even glancing up into the canopy, always checking for indications of the enemy.

At the breaks, he no longer collapsed to the ground as he had during the first one. That rest stop, though, had been in sight of the camp. Now that they were out in the jungle, Connel was aware of the danger. He sank to one knee, as the manuals suggested, and watched the jungle in front of him.

All of that impressed Fetterman. A new guy normally had to be told repeatedly that they were in a war zone. A new guy needed help learning how to survive in the jungle. Connel, on the other hand, acted like a veteran with three or four months under his belt. If he was as savvy in a firefight as he was in jungle survival, he would turn into a hell of a soldier. Fetterman wondered if he shouldn't suggest that Connel put in for the Special Forces. They could always use a good man, one with the intelligence to survive in the jungle.

Without a word the men slowly slipped along the top of the ridge and then over it, moving down toward the valley, but only ten feet or so to avoid being silhouetted against the sky.

Fetterman didn't have to brief the strikers as they slipped into position to ambush the enemy. The point-man had found the best spot, and the rest of the patrol filled in along a line. Two men slipped to the rear to protect the patrol from counterattack, while the men at either end of the line faced into the jungle in case the enemy tried to flank them.

Everything about the patrol suggested professionalism. The men knew what they were doing. Connel knew what he was doing. Fetterman, as an adviser, as the man along to make sure no mistakes were made, felt like a fifth wheel. With so many South Vietnamese soldiers incompetent and so many American infantry officers with insufficient training, it was good to find so many in one place who knew what to do.

Fetterman settled down to watch the jungle around him and to memorize the trees, bushes, ferns and debris on the ground. It would be a long night, but then they all were during an ambush in the jungle.

He listened to the jungle sounds, but there was nothing unusual. A light breeze blew through, rattling the leaves above him, but it wasn't enough to cover the sounds of approaching enemy soldiers, should such an event transpire. In fact, Fetterman was beginning to think the enemy wouldn't be coming.

But just then one of the strikers approached, stopped and leaned close. "Somebody come."

Fetterman nodded. "Let's be alert. I'll fire first, then everyone opens up."

"I tell others."

"You do that." Fetterman touched the safety of his weapon and made sure it was off. Then he touched a grenade hanging on his shoulder harness, making sure it was still there, though he knew it was. When the enemy came, if they did, Fetterman would use the grenade to start the fight.

11

JUNGLE NORTH OF BANG RON

Fetterman heard them coming long before he saw them. The jungle and the night concealed them, but words, quiet words in Vietnamese, told him all he needed to know. The enemy was scouring the ridges around the valley, making sure that the Americans and South Vietnamese hadn't stumbled onto the camp.

Fetterman pulled the grenade from his harness and put a finger through the loop of the pin. Then, turning his head slowly, he searched for enemy soldiers. At that moment a single shape loomed up out of the dark shadows, and Fetterman saw the AK in the man's hands.

He jerked the pin free and turned slightly, throwing the grenade like a center fielder trying to peg a man at home plate. He heard the grenade sail through the jungle and smash into the undergrowth.

"Grenade!" he called out, alerting his men. An instant later he heard the detonation, and shrapnel tore through the trees and bushes. A high-pitched wail indicated that someone had been wounded by the deadly metal.

Then firing erupted, both M-16s and AKs. The jungle was alive with flashes of light. A couple of detonations marked grenades thrown by his strikers. Then there were dull pops as the enemy responded with Chicom weapons.

"To the right!" yelled Connel.

Fetterman whirled, but there was nothing to see. Too much vegetation in his way.

"Come on," ordered Connel. "You're on me. Let's move it right now."

Fetterman didn't want to break up the integrity of the unit. At night, in the jungle, it was important that everyone stay where they were. It was too easy to get separated.

"Hold your positions!" ordered Fetterman.

A burst of fire from an AK no more than fifteen feet away singed the vegetation near Fetterman. He dropped down and fired upward into the muzzle-flash of the enemy weapon. A second burst slammed into the canopy overhead as the man fell back, screaming.

Fetterman got to his feet, but remained in a crouch. He blinked at the light show around him. The opposing forces were now trying to outguess each other. One M-16 fired, and two AKs answered it, the tracers lancing through the jungle. Fetterman put a burst into the muzzle-flash of one of them, and there was a crash in the jungle as a man behind it fell.

Fetterman then dropped down. He heard more rounds snap overhead. Rolling to the left, he got up on his knees and scanned the jungle, searching for a target in the night.

"We've got them on the run!" Connel shouted. "After them!"

"Hold!" yelled Fetterman. He turned toward the sound of the shouting, but he couldn't tell if Connel had listened to him or not.

CONNEL DIDN'T LIKE to fight at night. He was afraid to shoot, knowing his muzzle-flash would pinpoint his location. He wanted to use his grenades but was afraid they'd get hung up in the vegetation and detonate too close to him. Everything he could do to fight back would make him a target for the enemy.

In training no one had told him that. He knew the mechanics of an ambush. He knew how to set them and how to spring them. But no one had told him that muzzle-flashes, nearly invisible in the daytime, would be so bright at night. They lighted up the jungle like the flickering of an old-fashioned movie. He could see everything around him in the strobing as rounds were fired.

Aiming at the center of an enemy's muzzle-flash, he pulled the trigger. Just once. A single round. But it was answered by a burst from someone else who, thankfully, missed.

Tracers. That was something he hadn't thought about, either. Tracers in a firefight marked you as quickly as the muzzle-flash. Tracers were important. They helped you aim. Tracers could be used to mark enemy positions for the rest of the squad.

Connel had ignored the tracers, but now he saw them flashing all around him. Green ones from the VC and red ones from the strikers. He saw them hit, bounce and tumble upward to disappear in the canopy. The jungle was alive with tracers. Hundreds of them.

Connel rolled to the right, but still didn't fire. He saw a couple of shapes break away from the main body of the enemy and head off to his right. He came up on his knees and someone fired. The ground all around the shooter was bright with the muzzle-flash, and Connel could see the banana clip that marked an AK and an enemy soldier.

"To the right!" he shouted. He spotted a couple of the strikers and leaped to his feet. "Come on. You're on me. Let's move it right now."

"Hold your positions!" yelled Fetterman.

Connel slipped down then. There was movement behind him, his left. He popped up, fired and dropped down before he had a chance to see what happened.

The firing shifted, moving to his left. Through gaps in the vegetation, he could see the strobing of the weapons. One tracer hit a tree and fell to the ground, continuing to burn for a moment.

Another group of the enemy broke off and started running. One turned and fired, letting loose with the whole magazine. But the rounds were all high, missing everything.

Connel was up again, yelling, "We've got them on the run! After them!"

"Hold!" yelled Fetterman.

But Connel knew better. Once you had the advantage, you followed through. You didn't hold if the enemy was running. He could see that it was a rout, not a retreat. There was no organization to it. The enemy was getting out and now was the time to chase them.

Connel was up on his feet. He found three of the strikers and shouted at them, "Come with me!" He ran by them, stopped long enough to make sure they were following, then pressed on into the jungle.

That was the thing with the South Vietnamese. You couldn't trust them at all except to fuck you over. He had to make sure they were following him. Americans would have been up and running instantly.

He leaped over a fallen log and saw shapes in front of him. Dropping to one knee, his rifle butt against his hip, he fired a short burst, then another, longer one. The rounds tore through the jungle and connected. One man screeched and went down. Another tried to jump, was caught in the back and thrown forward. He didn't make a sound.

"Let's get them!" cried Connel. He was up and running again. Behind him he heard the strikers calling to one another. He heard them running and knew they would stick with him.

The ground dropped away sharply. He stumbled and fell to one knee and threw out his hands to break the fall. His left hand slipped in the soft, moist vegetation and he landed on his face and belly. Pain flared and the jungle was suddenly bright white. For a moment he couldn't see anything, though he could hear everything.

From the front came a sudden burst of fire. A machine gun and not an AK. A second joined the first, hammering away. Tracers lanced out and disappeared—bright green lights that looked as big as baseballs.

Suddenly Connel was scared. Fetterman had been right. He should have stayed where he was. Now he was somewhere down the hill and Fetterman didn't know where he was.

The muzzle-flash from the machine gun was to his left, maybe twenty feet away. Maybe more. In the jungle, at night, he couldn't tell. And he didn't care. The important thing now was to get out.

Twisting around, he began to crawl away from the machine gun, away from the enemy. Figuring that climbing back up the slope would kill him, he paralleled it, staying level, but moving away. He listened to the sounds behind him—M-16s and AKs firing at one another. Long bursts. Short bursts. Single shots. Grenades.

Glancing over his shoulder, he saw the jungle alive with fire, flickering and flashing everywhere. Tracers spun out of control. There were detonations from grenades, great rolling bangs followed by a downpour of debris and a cascade of deadly shrapnel.

Connel no longer cared about that. He had to get out. He stayed flat, reaching out with his hands as if trying to pull himself forward. He found a teak tree, the roots sticking up through the ground like the cradling fingers of a giant. He crawled in among them for the protection they offered. Then he turned and looked back, but the tiny firefight had ended.

FETTERMAN CRAWLED to his left past the body of a striker and into a shallow depression. He listened to the ebb and flow of the fight. Then, grenade in hand, he popped up, glanced and threw it at the first muzzle-flash he saw.

The detonation seemed to mark the end of the firefight. A couple of AKs speared the night air, but then fell silent. The M-16s continued to hammer, the rounds tearing into the jungle, but there was no enemy response.

Fetterman let it continue for a moment, then yelled, "Cease fire! Cease fire!"

When the last of the echoes died away, he listened to the jungle. Now there were almost no sounds. The birds, monkeys and everything else had been chased from the area by the sudden noise and danger. They knew enough to get out while the shooting was going on.

Fetterman slipped along the line of strikers, checking on them. He found one dead and another hurt. The Vietnamese was sitting on the ground, his rifle next to him as he tried to tie a bandage around his bleeding thigh. He seemed unaware of anything going on around him.

"You okay?" asked Fetterman.

The man looked up, his face a mask of pain. He was bathed in sweat and moaning softly, deep in his throat.

Fetterman pushed the man's hands away and looked at the wound. Blood was pouring from it. The bandage was already soaked. Fetterman tried to adjust the bandage, and as he did, there was a spurt of blood. The artery had been hit. It hadn't been severed, because the man would have died in seconds, but it had been nicked, and from the arc of blood that had splashed out, Fetterman knew there was nothing he could do.

"Lie down," he told the striker as he tried to adjust the bandage. But the man suddenly stiffened, and the master sergeant knew the Vietnamese was dead.

Fetterman left the body and moved down the line. He found two more strikers, unhurt, and ready in case the VC returned.

When he reached the end of the line, he found that it had been abandoned. Connel and a couple of the strikers were supposed to be there, protecting the flank, but he couldn't find any trace of them. He knew Connel had led them down the slope, chasing the fleeing VC. He stopped and looked. Even in the dark he could see the path they'd taken. It wasn't obvious, but it was visible, leading down into the valley. But there was no firing down there. They'd either missed the enemy, or they'd been ambushed in return. Fetterman didn't know which, and he wasn't going to pursue it in the dark.

Turning, he retraced his steps and worked his way to the other end of the line, where he found another wounded man who had bandaged himself. Pulling the line together, Fetterman had them withdraw to the south, two hundred yards from where they'd been.

"We have wounded," protested one of the strikers. "We must get them out."

Fetterman nodded. "But they're in no danger now. We need to hang in here."

"Wounded should be evacked."

"Yes," agreed Fetterman, "but it's only an hour to sunrise. We can't get a chopper in until then."

"Then we go," said the striker. "We go back to the camp. Must help wounded."

"No," said Fetterman. "We have people missing. We can't pull out until we have them located."

The striker sat there for a moment, thinking. "Sun come in one hour."

"And none of the wounded are in danger of dying soon," said Fetterman. "We need to wait here. Until morning. Until first light."

CONNEL STAYED THERE, cradled in the fingers of the tree, waiting to see what would happen next. The firing all around had tapered off, then stopped. The VC had pulled back, passing close to where he was hiding, but they hadn't seemed interested in searching for him.

As soon as they were farther down the slope, Connel stood up. Slowly he surveyed the jungle around him, but all motion, all sound, had disappeared. He reached up slowly and wiped the sweat from his face. Suddenly he realized he was thirsty. Extremely thirsty. Overwhelmingly thirsty.

Carefully, remembering that quick motion in the jungle drew attention, he pulled out his canteen. He opened it, lifted it to his lips and took a single swallow. It wasn't the best water in the world—it was warm and tasted of plastic and chemicals—but it was wet. Connel took another drink and then another, telling himself over and over that he'd had enough until he finished off the canteen.

He put it away, thought about the second one he carried, but knew there would be no stopping if he started on it, too. So he left it alone. Then he checked his rifle. Pulling out the partial magazine, he replaced it with a fully loaded one, then put the used one in his pocket. It would be the last magazine he would use if he ran into trouble.

He moved around the tree and felt his way along it, stopping on the other side and kneeling there. Again he surveyed the jungle and listened. He knew the enemy was gone. He knew he was alone there.

For a moment he thought he should try to find the strikers who had come with him. They were out there somewhere, but he decided they weren't worth it. It wasn't as if they were American soldiers. Besides, it was their country. If they had been good soldiers, they would have been looking for him.

The thing to do was to climb the hill and get to the top. From there he could slip down the other side, and if worse came to worst, find his way back to camp. All he had to do was put the ridge between him and the enemy.

He took a single step, stopped, listened, then took another. Slowly he continued uphill, staying low, trying to slip through the vegetation without making a noise.

When he reached the top of the ridge, he stopped again and crouched, listening to the jungle, trying to see into it. But without the sun it was impossible. Nothing but charcoal grays and jet blacks. And no sound. No insects buzzing. No animals calling. Nothing but the silence of death.

Connel stayed there for a moment, wondering what to do, his stomach flopping around like a dying fish. He'd dreamed of combat since he was old enough to understand it, and now he found himself in the thick of it. But it wasn't the adventure he had imagined. Now all he wanted was to get out.

In the morning.

That was all he had to do. Wait until morning and he would have a war story to tell everyone.

If he made it.

12

CARASEL HOTEL
SAIGON

Gerber sat in the chair of his hotel room, a bottle of Beam's in his hand. Morrow sat on the bed, dressed in a short skirt, light blouse and black shoes. She was leaning back, watching every move Gerber made.

Finally she said, "What in hell's going on here?"

"Going on?" asked Gerber, trying to sound innocent. "Going on where?"

"Here. Around here. You're in and out of Saigon. Here one minute, gone the next. When there's that much activity, there has to be something going on."

Gerber took a pull at the bourbon and exhaled. "That's smooth." He handed the bottle to Morrow and asked, "This on the record or off?"

She took a drink, then set the bottle on the floor near the bed and locked eyes with him. "You know better than that. What do you think?"

Gerber leaned back and laced his fingers behind his head. He stared at her for a moment, thinking that she was an awfully good-looking woman. A smart woman. A loyal woman.

But then, as a reporter, she was also one of the enemy. Gerber didn't know how the situation had developed, but it did exist. The American press, in their eagerness to get a story, had turned against the American soldier in Vietnam. They seemed to be going out of their way to make it harder for the soldier. They kept publishing stories that blurred the distinction between fact and fiction.

And Robin was a journalist. But then she had demonstrated she could be trusted. She was a fine reporter who didn't have an inflated sense of her own worth. She knew the score.

"On the record, everything's cool," he said. "Enemy activity is way down. Not much happening anywhere."

"And off the record?" she asked, retrieving the bottle for another drink.

"There seems to be a buildup northwest of here. We don't know why, but we know it's there."

"So what are you going to do?"

"Tonight? Nothing. Tomorrow? I'm going back out there and talk to Tony."

"Can I go?"

"I don't think so," said Gerber.

"I could talk to General Davies and be on a chopper in two hours."

"Not out to where I'm going," said Gerber. "Not tomorrow, anyway."

"Why?"

"Too dangerous."

"Oh, bullshit," said Morrow.

"No," said Gerber. "We don't need to get a reporter killed out there. Not now. Not with all the bad press we're already getting."

That stopped her for a moment. She set the bottle down and moved forward so that she was closer to him. "I don't like the direction this conversation is taking. I find it condescending."

Gerber took a deep breath and rubbed a hand through his hair. "Then I haven't made my position clear. I don't mean to be condescending. I only mean that we don't know what we have out there. And my reasons for keeping you out are of a personal nature."

"Worried about me?"

Gerber shrugged, then laughed. "Yeah. You could say that."

She started to move toward him, then stopped. Looking at him, she asked, "Then what's going on out there that causes you to worry?"

"I don't know," said Gerber. "We've got something going on, but I don't know what or how big it is. We're trying to find out now."

"I can accept that," she said. "But I'd like to get out there and look around."

"Give me a couple of days and then we'll see about getting you into the field."

She stood up. "Okay, a few days, but then I want to know the whole deal."

"If I ever find out, you'll be the first to know." He grinned. "One of the first, anyway."

"Fine." Slowly she began to unbutton her blouse. She shrugged out of it and let it fall to the floor. "I assume I'll be staying the night."

"You can count on it."

WHEN GERBER SLIPPED from the bed, it was still dark out. He stepped to the window quietly, softly, and looked down on the street. The neon still flashed and the crowds still circulated. Anytime of the day or night the crowds were there. Even during the Tet attacks the crowds had been there. Then they had been scurrying for cover. Now they were looking for pleasure, something to help them forget the war for a while.

"Wha's happening?" asked Morrow, propping herself on one elbow.

"Nothing," said Gerber. "Go back to sleep."

"You goin'?"

"In just a few minutes. I have to get back out into the field."

Now she was fully awake. She sat up. "What's the big hurry? You won't be able to get a chopper until sunrise."

Gerber turned from the window. "I just have to get moving. Even if I'm sitting around Hotel Three, at least it will seem that I'm doing something."

"I'll go over there with you."

Gerber shook his head. "Stay here. Sleep."

For a moment Morrow didn't move or speak. Then she said, "You call me the moment you get back?"

"Of course."

"Then good luck."

Gerber moved to the bathroom, turned on the light and entered. He took a quick shower, shaved, then grinned at himself in the mirror as he brushed his teeth. He was about to head out into the field, but he was going out clean and freshly shaved. He wouldn't offend the enemy with a filthy body or stubble on his chin.

Back in the other room, he dressed quickly and retrieved his rifle from the wardrobe. Ready, he knelt next to the bed. "I'm taking off," he whispered.

Morrow rolled over and looked up at him. "Be careful."

"I always am. Very careful, because I'm getting too old for this shit." He kissed her lightly.

"See you later, Mack."

He stood and looked down at her. She was barely visible in the half-light filtering through the window. Then he turned, walked to the door and let himself out. Downstairs he left his key at the front desk and walked out onto the street. The humidity hit him like a wet, sticky sledgehammer. Sweat beaded on his forehead and dripped down his sides in a matter of seconds.

He found his jeep, unlocked it and climbed behind the wheel. Driving toward Tan Son Nhut, he noticed the traffic had thinned. There weren't as many civilian vehicles on the road, but there seemed to be the same number of jeeps and trucks as always. The military never slept, even in a nine-to-five war.

At the gate to Tan Son Nhut, he was waved through by a sleepy MP who seemed to have lost his enthusiasm for his job. Gerber returned the jeep to the MACV-SOG building, left the key with a sergeant who was sitting in a dark room listening to the radios, then walked over to Hotel Three.

As the sun made its first appearance, just a thin band of pale gray on the horizon, Gerber entered the terminal. A single chopper was sitting on the field, its engine running, blades spinning.

"Can't get you all the way," said the clerk, "but that chopper's on its way to Tay Ninh."

"That'll do me fine," said Gerber. He turned and hurried from the building. The crew chief helped him on board, and as he buckled the seat belt, the aircraft lifted off.

THE NOISE LEVEL in the jungle was increasing. Fetterman knew that it meant the sun was rising. Through the triple canopy and dense vegetation, he couldn't see anything. The stars and moon were concealed, but the animals and birds could sense daybreak, and they greeted it with gusto. Fetterman was ready for morning. More than ready.

He moved along the line, checking each soldier. They had stayed put since they had withdrawn from the battle. He stopped to check the wounded. They were in good shape, considering. Fetterman knew they would be evacced to Tay Ninh before the day was over and that Suttin would complain once again about the way he and Gerber were whittling down his command.

"We find others?" asked one of the strikers quietly.

Fetterman nodded. "At first light we'll sweep the field for them."

"No sound. They dead."

"No," said Fetterman. "They're lying low, like we are. We'll get to them soon."

"Many VC here. More than we have soldiers at camp," said the striker.

Fetterman crouched by the man. "Why do you say that?"

"VC everywhere. Sneaking. Spying. VC come in night to kill soldiers at camp."

"Why do you say that?" Fetterman repeated.

"I know. We see. VC come to talk to our men. Try to make them leave camp."

"When?" asked Fetterman.

"Two days. Before families come into camp. VC warn that battle coming."

Fetterman could barely see the striker. He rubbed his chin with his hand and tried not to laugh. They had gone into the field a dozen times to look for the enemy. They had discussed the numbers and what the targets might be, but all along the strikers had known the score.

Fetterman knew the South Vietnamese, even those not sympathetic to the VC cause, were warned before big attacks. He'd been around enough of the large American bases to know the signs as well as anyone. If the workers didn't show, it meant something was going to happen. It meant that mortars or rockets were going to be fired. Americans, seeing that the South Vietnamese workers weren't coming in, were alerted. The VC might talk about how well their intelligence system warned them in advance of American sweeps, but the Americans had a system that was as good and as reliable.

"You should have said something sooner."

The striker shrugged, a gesture he'd seen the Americans use. "I just did."

Fetterman stood and finished his quick inspection. He'd learned a bit of intelligence that he wanted to share with Gerber and Suttin as soon as he could, but he didn't want the man to know how important the information was. Sometimes it was wiser to underplay the knowledge. That way more would be told at a later time.

Finished, Fetterman returned to his position at the end of the line. He listened as the noise around him increased. Flies and mosquitoes swarmed around him. Gnats darted in and out, tasting the salt from his sweat. But Fetterman didn't try to swat them. He ignored the pests and concentrated on the jungle around him.

Deep charcoal changed to light gray. Shapes that had been black and vague took on dimension and color. At first he could see two or three feet in front of him and then five and finally ten or twelve. The sun had risen, and the slanting rays were beginning to penetrate the thick vegetation.

It was time to begin the sweep. Fetterman stood and again walked down the line. The strikers formed around him. Pointing at two men, he said, "You wait here with the wounded and guard them. We'll be no more than an hour, then we'll head back to camp."

Neither man looked disappointed with the instructions. The rest of them were ready to go. They fanned out and began to climb to the top of the ridge again, moving slowly, watching the jungle, always listening.

Fetterman reached the crest and stopped. He held a hand up, then fell to one knee on the wet jungle carpet. He tried to see down into the valley, but the thick vegetation and wisps of morning fog blocked the view.

To the left, down the ridge, was the scene of the last firefight. Trees were stripped of bark and leaves. Bushes had been riddled by bullets. There was a buzz in the distance, like that of a saw in a lumber mill, as flies swarmed around the spilled blood of dead men.

The path taken by Connel and the other strikers wasn't immediately apparent, but Fetterman spotted it. It led down into the valley where the VC had congregated. He moved forward, stopped and listened.

To the right, farther down the ridge, came a quiet noise—a foot scraping the thick carpet. Fetterman turned and watched, waiting to see who would appear. The noise shifted then, as if the man had suddenly reached the top of the ridge, farther to the right. Fetterman touched the safety on his rifle, just to be sure, and stared into the jungle.

There was a flicker of movement. A branch snapped back into place. Then, near that, there was a flash, and Fetterman spotted the man. A moment later Connel stepped into view, not knowing he had exposed himself to Fetterman.

The master sergeant watched and waited, but there was no one with Connel and no one following him. The lieutenant was alone in the jungle. Fetterman stood, took a step and then froze. He didn't know Connel's state of mind and didn't want a frightened man to open fire before identifying his target. Too many soldiers had been killed by trigger-happy friends.

As Connel approached, Fetterman stepped forward and purposely snapped a twig. Connel froze but didn't spin or open fire. Fetterman grinned, then whispered, "We've got you covered, sir."

Connel dropped on all fours at the sound of the voice, then slowly got back onto his feet. He searched the area around him rapidly, trying to spot Fetterman.

"Coming to you, sir," said the master sergeant.

"Come ahead."

Fetterman stepped forward over a rotting log and into an open area where Connel could easily see him. "Are you hurt, sir?"

"No, I'm fine." He stepped toward Fetterman, lowering the barrel of his weapon as he did.

"The others?" asked Fetterman.

"Dead. They're dead."

"You're sure?"

Connel shrugged, as if to say he didn't know. "They're dead. I'm sure."

"You saw them?"

"What is this, Sergeant? I told you, they're dead."

Fetterman moved closer and lowered his voice. "We don't need to shout in the jungle."

"The enemy's gone," said Connel.

"You're sure of that, too?" asked Fetterman.

"Sergeant, I told you what I know. Those men are dead and the enemy has retreated down the hill. I saw them go. Saw them do it. That's why I was able to get out of there. Now I'd like to get back to the camp."

"We need to recover the bodies," said Fetterman.

"What in hell for? The men are dead. All of them are dead. There's no need to look for the bodies."

"Don't you know where they are?" asked Fetterman. "You said you saw them dead."

"Sergeant, this isn't the time nor the place for a debate. We have to get out of here."

Fetterman had to agree with that. He glanced at the strikers behind him and then back at Connel. He knew they should try to retrieve the bodies. It wasn't the grandstand play that some might believe it to be. It was a psychological factor. The South Vietnamese strikers were better soldiers when they knew their bodies would be properly buried when they died, if they knew that the enemy wouldn't mutilate them.

"We've got to get out of here," Connel said again.

Fetterman looked over the man's shoulder into the jungle, wondering if there was something chasing him. Then he looked at Connel. "You're sure they're dead?"

"Yes, damn it, they're fucking dead."

Thinking of the wounded, Fetterman nodded. "Then let's go." He whirled and looked into the face of one of the strikers. "We're getting out."

The man turned slowly and began working his way to the rear. Fetterman waited for Connel to pass him and then fell in as the rear guard. He noticed that Connel's uniform was torn and dirty. It looked as if the lieutenant had crawled through the jungle. But there was nothing to tell him if Connel was telling the truth. Nothing at all.

13

BANG RON CAMP

Fetterman stood near the tiny refrigerator, a cold Coke in his hand. He waved it once and said, "I need to get back out there and find the bodies."

"No," said Gerber. "You need to sit down and talk to us. The dead can wait."

Fetterman nodded and pulled out a chair. He dropped into it and wiped a hand over his face, which was covered with sweat. "Yes, sir."

"From the top," said Gerber. "Tell it all to me."

Fetterman took a drink of Coke and set the can down on the table. He glanced at Suttin and asked, "This new guy isn't a good friend of yours, is he?"

"Met him when you did," said Suttin.

"Okay. First things first. He's good in the jungle. Understands it in a way most men don't. He can move through it quietly and knows how to avoid making noise and showing himself. Not afraid of it either, like some. Knows the dangers and knows that most of them are overblown by the press and Hollywood producers."

"He impressed you," said Gerber.

"For a first-timer, yes, sir. I was impressed."

"But," said Gerber, knowing there was more.

"He hates the Vietnamese."

"How can you tell?" asked Suttin.

Fetterman faced the man. "Little things. Way he talks to them. Things he says about them. He thinks they're not worth much because we have to help them. We're fighting their war while they sit around Saigon, making a few bucks from the Americans and on the war."

"How long has he been in-country?" asked Gerber.

"A week, if that," said Suttin. "They pulled him out of Saigon, and when he checked in at brigade head-quarters, they passed him over to me."

"That was fairly quick," said Gerber.

"But the point," said Fetterman, "is his attitude. The strikers can pick it up, too. He's not going to be effective here if his attitude doesn't change."

"Which gets us back to the original point," said Gerber. "What about the strikers who followed him?"

"I suppose they're dead," said Fetterman, "but there was something about the way he said it that bothers me. I think he's making that assumption, but he doesn't know for sure no matter what he's saying. That's why I want to get back out into the field."

"No," said Gerber. "That's not possible."

"Why?"

Gerber glanced at Suttin and then back to Fetterman. "Heavy arty will be falling inside of an hour. There's no time to get in and out again."

"It won't be falling on that ridge," said Fetterman.

"Tony, you don't want to be anywhere near that ridge or valley when the bombs begin to fall. You've seen the results of a heavy arty strike. Hell, they don't have to hit you. All they have to do is come close."

Fetterman nodded. "The South Vietnamese aren't going to like that."

"Nothing we can do about it," said Gerber. "There comes a point when it's impossible to recover the remains of the dead, and we shouldn't sacrifice the living to do it."

"That's what I expected to hear from Connel. Especially if the dead are Vietnamese."

Gerber stared at his sergeant for a moment. "You're not suggesting that he left survivors out there, are you?"

"I hope not," said Fetterman. "I don't think so. Still, there was something funny about his attitude."

Gerber turned to Suttin. "If there are any Vietnamese in your strike force that you trust, you'd better get a reading on this. They might believe, rightly or wrongly, that Connel deserted their comrades and might decide to get even. You've got to get an answer quickly."

"I can make a few inquiries," said Suttin. "Is it really that important?"

"I've worked with the Vietnamese during two tours," said Gerber, "and the relationships you develop with them are the most important thing you do. If that gets screwed up, you create more VC. Treat them honestly, fairly and like human beings and they'll do whatever they can for you. Fuck with them and they'll eat you alive."

"Yes, sir," said Suttin.

Gerber looked at Fetterman. "Anything else?"

"Will we be hitting the field after the heavy arty?"

"They'll want someone to assess the damage, and we're right here to do it. I'm sure they'll want us to look things over."

"Then I'd like to get some sleep." He grinned at Gerber. "I didn't have the luxury of a night in Saigon."

"I didn't get much sleep," he said.

"But that was your own fault," Fetterman shot back as he stood up.

"You've got me there."

CONNEL STOPPED at the perimeter and looked back over the grassy field they'd just come through. He could see their path, marked through the elephant grass by the darker green of the vegetation. Standing there, hands cupped above his eyes to shade them, he searched the jungle, but saw nothing there other than birds.

Satisfied that no one had followed them and that no one would suddenly appear out there, he walked back toward his hootch. He ignored the Vietnamese around him, relegating them to the background like the trees, perimeter and hootches. He didn't like to listen to them jabbering at one another with that singsong language that was more of an irritation to him than a means of communication for them. He hated the way they spoke, hated the music they listened to and hated the things they ate. He had yet to find one thing about the Vietnamese that was appealing.

Connel entered his hootch and set his weapon in the corner without bothering to unload it. Crossing to his cot, he sat down and glanced at the doorway. In the bright sunlight outside he saw two Vietnamese strikers walk past. Neither looked in at him.

The strikers were dead, he told himself. He was sure they were dead. If they hadn't been, they would have made some noise out in the jungle. He would have heard or seen them. If they weren't dead, they would have gotten out.

Besides, it didn't matter. They were only Vietnamese. Stupid gooks who weren't worth the powder it would take to blow them up. If it had been American soldiers, he would have made certain they were dead before leaving them. If they had been Americans, they would have gotten themselves out.

Connel stood up and walked to the door. Outside, the families of the Vietnamese workers were beginning to walk around. There were men, women and children everywhere, along with oxen and chickens. The camp had been turned into a goddamn farm.

Connel shook his head. They all seemed so dirty. They didn't bathe. They thought nothing of squatting whenever the mood moved them. No concept of hygiene or cleanliness. They didn't know how to use a latrine or care to use it. A filthy people not worth the money that was being wasted on them. Incapable of understanding what was going on around them.

Connel turned and walked back into his hootch. He sat down on the cot, pulled off his boots and wondered how he had been condemned to this. In school, in ROTC, he had thought of war as high adventure. He'd been on his way to save democracy from communism. They had discussed the ways of war. He remembered talking about the Navy sub captain who had machine-gunned Japanese soldiers. That was the way to fight a war. Kill the enemy without mercy.

Now he was stuck in some out-of-the-way corner of Vietnam, surrounded by natives, and he didn't know who the enemy was. It could be any of the men or women, or hell, even the children around him. Any and all of them could be the enemy. He would be right to step to the door and open fire. Kill everyone with slanted eyes around him.

War wasn't the glorious adventure he had dreamed of, not when the allies were almost subhuman and incapable of fighting. He wouldn't be surprised if one of them tried to sneak into the hootch at night and cut his throat. That was the way the bastards fought and thought.

He lay back on the cot and wondered how long he would have to stay at Bang Ron before he could ask for a new assignment. A good one where he'd work with other Americans. Men he could trust to back him up in a fight. Good men who weren't afraid of gunfire and who knew how their weapons worked.

In the distance he heard a rumbling, a quiet, ominous sound that built slowly until his hootch shook. He sat up, wondering if it was an earthquake or some weather phenomenon he had yet to encounter. Christ, how he hated this country.

As FETTERMAN LEFT to catch some sleep, Gerber decided he would go and hang around the radio shack. He descended into the darkness and wondered why radio rooms were always dark. There was no reason for it. Radios didn't work better in the dark. It didn't make them easier to see, and yet all radio rooms were dark.

The coolness inside he understood. Radios did work better when kept cool. The heat and humidity of Vietnam could ruin a radio in a matter of hours. They had to be kept cool if possible.

And the bunkers were necessary. Radios were the lifeline that linked small camps with all the elements of rescue. Lose the radios and those links were cut. Camps could then be overrun. Radios were necessary, and soldiers made sure they were protected.

The man sitting next to the radios at this camp was an old soldier, maybe thirty-five. He was thin and had brown hair and a dark face. His feet were propped on a small table to the right of the rack of radios.

"Anything on the radios, Sergeant?" asked Gerber as he entered.

The man dropped his feet to the ground and turned to look. "No, sir. It's quiet."

And then, as if to contradict the sergeant, one of the speakers boomed, "Attention, all aircraft. Attention, all aircraft. I have a heavy arty advisory in effect until 1300 hours this afternoon. All aircraft are advised to remain more than five nautical miles from grid coordinates X ray tango nine-one-five-four-two-two, falling through thirty-three thousand feet. I say again, all aircraft are advised to remain more than five nautical miles from grid coordinates X ray tango nine-one-five-four-two-two, falling through thirty-three thousand feet. Heavy arty advisory out."

"You get that?" asked Gerber.

"Yes, sir." The sergeant stood up and moved to the table. He sorted through the maps and opened one. Moving a finger along it, he said, "Here. Right about here."

Gerber checked the map and saw that the valley he and Fetterman had explored was in the middle of the five-mile radius. Maxwell had been as good as his word. They weren't going to take any chances with the VC this time.

"Thanks," said Gerber.

He climbed out of the commo bunker and glanced up at the sky, shading his eyes, but he couldn't see the airplanes. Heavy arty meant B-52s. Probably three of them.

Gerber walked over to the fire control tower and looked up at it. He shrugged and began to climb the ladder. When he reached the platform at the top, he stepped over the sandbags that protected it and found a PRC-25, a field phone and a pair of binoculars. Grabbing the latter, he lifted them to his eyes and scanned the sky but saw nothing.

He turned the binoculars on the jungle. From the tower he could see the paths Suttin's patrols had made as they'd moved from the gate and out into the jungle. All of them seemed to converge at one point. He'd have to tell Suttin about that. It would be too easy for the enemy to set up a future ambush. Trails had to be varied. Predictability invited disaster.

He scanned the jungle again, but there was nothing interesting going on. Shadows danced through treetops. Monkeys chased one another. Birds windmilled overhead, diving and soaring.

Then, suddenly, far to the east, there was a flash of light. Gerber turned, and with the powerful binoculars, could just make out three specks flying formation. He watched them grow slowly, taking on shape, and wondered if the VC or NVA were paying any attention to them. The bombers flew so high that Charlie couldn't do anything about them. And by the time he had them spotted, he couldn't run. The bombs would either fall on him or they wouldn't.

The B-52s came on relentlessly in the clear blue sky. Then, unexpectedly, they turned, as if they had been ordered back at the last moment. Gerber knew there was no reason for them to turn without dropping their bombs. There had been no firing from the ground, nothing to chase them away.

They turned north, then east, flying away from the valley and the enemy. And just as Gerber was beginning to believe they hadn't dropped their bombs, he heard the distant rumbling, felt it in the soles of his feet as the bombs detonated in the valley where the VC were hiding.

The noise went on and on as the bombs detonated, tearing up the ground. Heavy bombs. Five hundred pounders that would have been called blockbusters in another war. Maybe even some thousand pounders to shake up the enemy, to crush the tunnels Charlie might have built to avoid the Americans.

The tower vibrated with each impact. The Vietnamese strikers on the ground had stopped moving and were staring into the distance, trying to figure out what was happening. They were all facing north, where the bombers had been. Then one of them pointed at the sky.

Suttin came out of his office and glanced at the sky north of the camp. Then he turned and looked up at Gerber. "That it?"

"That's it."

"Shit."

Gerber crouched, put the binoculars into their case, then climbed over the sandbag wall and down the ladder. He walked over to Suttin. "We need to get some patrols organized to survey the damage."

"How many?"

"Three good-size ones set up to support one another if they need it. One to work as reinforcements and two to search the bomb zone."

"How soon?"

"The quicker the better," said Gerber. "One night in the field." He laughed. "Poor Tony's going to have to stay awake another night."

"Why not leave Sergeant Fetterman here? I'll take one patrol. Lieutenant Connel can have the reserve, and you can take the last one. Fetterman can control from the commo bunker in the compound."

"Sure," said Gerber. "That would work."

"How soon do you want to move out?" Suttin asked.

"Let me check in with Saigon, and if we're clear, we should be able to head out in an hour or so. Certainly no more than that."

"Yes, sir."

"Oh," said Gerber, "we'll want to vary our route into the jungle. I noticed that everything was focused on one location."

"No problem."

Gerber glanced up at the sun and then at his watch. He wiped the sweat from his face with the sleeve of his jungle fatigues. "It's going to be miserable moving through the heat of the day, but it'll be good to get this over with sooner."

Suttin followed his gaze. "Yes, sir. How many men will be going out?"

"Three patrols of twenty-five strikers each, each with radios and in contact with one another. If the bombers did their job, Charlie's going to be in sad shape and it'll be a cakewalk. If they missed, Charlie's going to be royally pissed."

"Then we'll want to be ready."

"More than ready," said Gerber. He hesitated, then said, "I'll meet you back here in thirty minutes. You alert Connel and I'll get with Fetterman."

"Thirty minutes," said Suttin. He turned and trotted across the compound.

14

BANG RON

They sat around the table in the team house with a map spread out in front of them. Gerber pointed at the valley to the north and said, ''They should have dropped the bombs along here. If they followed the standard procedure, the bomb line will be about a mile long and a couple of hundred yards wide. The craters will be thirty or forty feet deep.''

''Just what are we looking for?'' asked Connel.

Gerber rubbed a hand over his face. ''We're looking to see if the bombs did any good. We're looking for damage. We're looking for the dead. We're looking for broken equipment.''

''We'll be able to see that?'' asked Connel.

''You'll have to look,'' said Suttin. ''Look for signs. The more you see, the more obvious it is, the more damage the planes did.''

''Body count,'' said Connel. ''How do we handle that?''

''Two feet equals one body,'' said Gerber.

''What?''

Gerber waved a hand. "Don't worry about getting an exact count. The statistics the brass hats and the press are so fond of don't mean anything. We've been told we can count weapons as bodies. The feeling in Saigon is that a soldier would never throw his weapon away. The only way to get it away from the soldier is to kill him."

"Shit," said Suttin.

"You hadn't heard that?" asked Gerber.

"Not that one. I've gotten some of the other instructions. Body parts count. That sort of thing."

Connel looked from Gerber to Suttin. "Are there really instructions like that?"

"Certainly," said Gerber. "We want an accurate measure of the progress of the war. The generals need to be able to tell the politicians that the war's being fought and won. Dead men are as good a measure as any other. The kill ratio is something like eight or nine to one."

"Shit," said Connel.

Gerber touched the map again. "Connel, you'll want to set up along the ridge here. Lieutenant Suttin and I will proceed down into the valley for the search. You'll have to be alert to where we are and what's going on down there. You might be called to help."

"Yes, sir."

"And if we have no trouble, we'll retreat to you. All three units will form and then we'll come back here. Questions?"

Suttin studied the map, then asked, "Why not have choppers make the survey?"

"Because we can do a better job. We can pick up insignia, papers and equipment. We can get a better feel for it," said Gerber.

"Yeah," said Suttin. "I just wish someone else could do it."

"Understood," said Gerber. "Anything else?" Gerber looked at both men. "Okay. We'll meet by the gate in an hour, ready to move."

The meeting broke up then. Gerber watched both men leave and then stood up. He walked out into the bright light and stood there for a moment, remembering what Fetterman had said about Connel. He walked across the compound and found the hootch where Fetterman was sleeping. The master sergeant had taken off his shirt and hung it on the back of a wooden chair. His rifle was near the edge of the bed, within easy reach.

From the door, Gerber said, "Sergeant?" He knew better than to walk up and tap Fetterman's shoulder.

Fetterman didn't move, but said, "Yes?"

Gerber stepped into the hootch. "We're going out again to check the B-52 strike."

Fetterman sat up and rubbed his face. He groaned. "I'm getting too old for this shit, Captain. What time is it?"

"You've been asleep for about two hours."

"Christ."

"We're going out again. Suttin, Connel and I are taking three patrols. You'll stay here and run things."

"No, sir. I'll go out with you. Leave Connel here."

"Tony, you haven't had a good night's sleep in a week. It'll be better if you stay here."

"Connel isn't that good. By himself, in the jungle, he's okay, but not running a unit."

"He's an infantry officer. He knows how to do it."

"Captain, do you really believe that? Sure, he probably knows the book and knows how to set things up, but isn't there something more to it? Isn't there some finesse that can be brought into play? Two officers go out to set up ambushes. One always hits and the other rarely does.

Why? Because he understands things on a basic level. He's connected in some way that we don't understand. It's finesse."

Gerber leaned back against the door frame and stared at Fetterman. He knew the sergeant was right. There were officers, soldiers, who understood their business on a level that most never attained. There were surgeons with the gift. Or ball players. Or even journalists. People who instinctively understood how to do the job. Fetterman was one of those. He sensed things that others didn't.

"There comes a time," said Gerber finally, "when the finesse isn't what's needed. I can't see Connel getting into trouble on the ridge, but I can see something happening to you after a week in the field with hardly any sleep."

"Sir, I think you're the one making the mistake."

"So you've said."

Fetterman took a deep breath. "Connel's a racist."

"Now what in hell does that mean?"

"He hates the Vietnamese," said Fetterman. "Really, passionately, hates them. That's going to get in his way out in the field."

"There's a lot of racism here. Americans who hate the Vietnamese and Vietnamese who hate the Americans. North Vietnamese hate the South Vietnamese. It doesn't have to affect the job being done."

Fetterman shook his head, realizing finally that he had lost the fight. Gerber wasn't going to change his mind. It was one of the few times the captain had refused to listen to the voice of reason.

"Captain, I'm not that tired. One more night won't make that much difference."

"Tony, we're not going to be that far out. If we need help, you'll be able to provide it. If I had any reservations about this, I'd make some changes."

"It's a mistake, Captain."

"That's enough, Sergeant."

Fetterman shot Gerber a glance and knew the discussion was finally over. "Yes, sir."

"We'll be moving out in about an hour."

"I'll be there," said Fetterman.

"EVERYTHING SET?" asked Gerber.

"We're ready," said Suttin.

Gerber wanted to inspect the troops, but felt he would be insulting Suttin, who had been at the camp for a long time and had done a good job without the help of anyone except the strikers. Fetterman appeared then. He glanced at the lines of Vietnamese strikers, then walked up to Gerber. "You ready to pull out?"

"In a couple of minutes."

"I'll be standing by in the commo bunker," Fetterman said.

"I don't think you need to wait there."

"Well, it's cooler and quieter, and I'll probably be able to catch up on some sleep."

"Whatever," said Gerber.

"We're ready to go," Suttin said.

"You first," Gerber said. "Then Connel's bunch. I'll bring up the rear. Remember, we want to vary our route out to the jungle."

"Yes, sir." Suttin wheeled and walked back to his squad. He conferred with one of the NCOs, and then one man hurried through the gate. As that man reached the runway, the rest of the patrol began to filter out.

When the first patrol was through, Connel ordered his men forward. They stopped near the gate, watched as Suttin's people spread out in the field of elephant grass, then began to exit.

"Good luck, Captain," said Fetterman. "Remember what I told you about Connel."

"I'll keep it in mind, Tony."

Without a word from Gerber, one of the NCOs headed for the gate. He stopped there, waved one man through and then the strikers began to move.

"Normal check-in times," said Gerber.

"Understood, Captain."

"I'll see you tomorrow."

"Yes, sir."

Gerber joined the men. As they left the camp, one of the remaining defenders closed the gate. Gerber stopped at the edge of the runway and watched the men from the first two patrols spread out, trying to avoid the rendezvous point in the jungle that had been used in the past.

Gerber ordered his men forward, and when they reached the jungle they halted. Suttin and his men were off to the left. Gerber knew where they were. Connel was between him and Suttin. They had made three small penetrations into the jungle and had stopped.

But Suttin didn't sit around for long. He ordered his men up and moving. Connel and his patrol fell in behind them, a hundred yards to the rear, but following in their footsteps.

Gerber let them get deeper into the jungle and then ordered his men forward, paralleling the path of the first two units. With his flankers out, he felt it would be impossible for them to all walk into an ambush. They were in position to support one another if something went wrong.

For the next couple of hours they worked their way through the jungle and up the slope. With the sun directly overhead, the jungle heated up rapidly, so they took frequent breaks. The air was dead still, making the humidity even harder to bear.

By the time they reached the top of the ridge, the men were bushed. They fanned out, collapsed onto the ground and waited for their orders. Gerber moved to the RTO, took the handset and pressed it to his ear. "Zulu Five, this is Six."

"Go, Six," said Fetterman a moment later.

"First checkpoint."

"Roger."

"Break, break. Headhunter Six, this is Zulu Six."

"Go," said Suttin.

"We're in position and ready to begin the sweep as outlined."

"Roger, Zulu Six. We're in place, too."

"Break, break. Headhunter Five, this is Zulu Six."

"Go."

"Say status."

"Roger, Six, we're set up and ready to go," said Connel.

Gerber checked his watch. "We'll begin the sweep in one-zero minutes."

"This is Headhunter Six. Roger."

"Five rogers."

Gerber gave the handset back to the RTO. Then he pointed at an NCO and said, "We go in ten minutes."

"Yes, sir."

Gerber crouched and tried to see down into the valley. Nothing was visible to him, but that didn't matter. In a few minutes he would know what faced them.

15

IN THE JUNGLE NORTH
OF BANG RON

As they moved down the slope into the valley, there were no signs of bombing. But as they got closer to the valley floor, subtle changes became evident. An eerie silence hung in the air. And they could smell an overwhelming stench, a nauseating combination of acrid cordite and slaughterhouse butchery.

Gerber led the patrol now, having taken the point. He moved slowly, deliberately, searching the jungle around him. The vegetation still seemed to be intact. There were no signs of shrapnel or bullet damage. Then they saw a thin layer of shredded leaves littering the ground like the paper fallout of a ticker tape parade. Light clouds of dust and smoke drifted quietly through the jungle.

The jungle itself changed from a dim green hothouse to a bright open area. They came out of the trees and into a lunar landscape. As far as they could see, the ground had been churned, ripped up and tossed around. Now the mustiness of an open grave washed over them—fresh soil baked under a sun that had been invisible only a few hours earlier.

"Jesus," said Gerber. He'd seen what heavy arty could do before, but nothing like this. He held up a hand to halt the strikers, then knelt at the edge of the bomb strikes. Craters thirty, forty, maybe fifty feet across, stretched out as far as he could see. Smoke rose from some of them. Jungle vegetation that had been too wet to burn that morning was now ash, superheated in the detonations of the huge bombs. The ground had been scorched, blackened in places. Poles that had once been tree trunks were tilted at strange angles. Shattered limbs, stripped of leaves, hung awkwardly, pointing at the ground. Small trees lay around the craters, pointing outward like the spokes of a wheel.

It was an awesome display of firepower. Finally Gerber stood up and moved forward. He left the protection of the jungle and walked to the edge of the first crater. There was a ridge of earth around it, four or five feet high. Stepping up, he looked down, judging the hole to be at least forty feet deep. The sides of the crater were steep, and a pool of water was beginning to form at the bottom.

Stepping away from the crater, he moved along the line. Behind him the Vietnamese strikers filtered out of the jungle. Some of them looked down into the crater. Others avoided it as if it were bad medicine or black magic.

Gerber was now searching for signs of the enemy, anything that would tell him that the destruction had been done for a reason. He stopped once and looked up at the blue sky. A single bird soared on the air currents, its wings flapping occasionally.

He moved on, and as he did, the strikers spread out around him. They walked toward the center of the moonscape, moving cautiously. It seemed the bombers had missed everything of importance. Once again they had bombed the jungle but not the enemy.

SUTTIN STOOD on an outcropping of rock and looked down at the line of bomb craters. Directly below him lay the body of a dead Vietcong. It was dressed in black pajamas and looked to be in perfect shape, except that the head was missing. There didn't seem to be any blood around it, just the body, complete with a pistol belt and canteen.

Suttin retreated and rejoined his men. Without a word he moved down around the outcropping and out onto the valley floor. He stopped almost immediately, looking down at another body, this one in khaki. Blood was flowing from the dead man's mouth, nose, ears and eyes. He looked strangely shrunken, as if the life had been sucked out of him.

With the strikers spread out behind him, Suttin moved deeper into the zone of destruction. At the edge of some of the craters, and between them, were the remains of underground bunkers and tunnels. There were openings in the sides of some of the craters, like giant wormholes. A few of them had broken equipment in them, while the bottoms of some of the craters held shattered bodies.

Suttin, along with his patrol, moved along, taking it all in. They saw twisted rifles, a dented canteen, an entrenching tool with a broken handle. Some of the debris was partially buried, and some of it lay on the ground as if it had been placed there earlier for an inspection.

"Bombs did the job," said the NCO.

Suttin glanced at him and was surprised by the look on his face. Suttin was slightly sickened by the destruction. In his mind he could imagine the fear the Vietcong must have felt as the ground around them had erupted into fire and flame and fountains of dirt. The sky had dropped death on them and they had been trapped like rats.

But the NCO seemed to be pleased with all the destruction. Maybe that was born of sitting in mud hootches while the VC slipped into his village during the night to collect taxes and draft the young. Maybe the striker had seen friends die and had been powerless to do anything. Maybe he felt the VC were getting everything they deserved, no matter how terrible it was.

"Let's keep moving. Everyone stay alert," ordered Suttin.

"Yes, sir," said the NCO.

They fanned out among the craters, taking stock of everything they could see. Suttin picked up a rifle with a hole in the stock. He thought of the body count rules. This meant another dead soldier, though there was no body near it. Ten feet away there was a foot in a sandal, chopped off at the ankle with surgical precision. White bone glistened in the late-afternoon sun.

Another body, even if it was only a foot. Maybe one foot equals a body, thought Suttin. A rifle and a foot. Two bodies or one? And did it really matter?

He finally sat down on a tree trunk and shook his head. He couldn't take it anymore. Couldn't stand looking at the broken bodies of the dead.

CONNEL STAYED in position on the ridge for nearly thirty minutes, then decided he couldn't take it any longer. The war, the fighting, the searching was going on below him, and he was being left out of it. If medals were to be won, if glory was to be gained, then it would happen below on the valley floor. Whoever heard of winning medals and gaining glory by sitting around in the backup role? It was the men in the field of play who got their names in the paper. The men who warmed the bench were never mentioned.

Connel pointed at five men, senior men, men who had more military training than the others. "I want you to come with me." Then, thinking about it, he pointed at the senior NCO. "You stay. You're in charge."

"Yes, sir."

"You wait here with the radio. Anything happens, you'll have to take care of it."

"Yes, sir."

"Don't move from this spot," said Connel. He wanted to make the instructions clear so that even a stupid Vietnamese could understand them. "You stay and we'll return in an hour or so. I just want to take a look below us."

"Stay here," said the Vietnamese NCO.

"Right."

"Yes, sir."

Connel stood up, thought about the extra weight of his pistol belt and unbuckled it, dropping it onto the ground. "Watch the equipment."

"Yes, sir."

With the four men he'd picked, Connel started down the slope. Since both Gerber and Suttin had gotten head starts, he moved faster, veering to the east. He wanted to get to the far end of the bomb craters and sweep in from the other direction. If there were any VC left alive, he'd be in position to either chase them toward Gerber and Suttin or kill them if they ran in the opposite direction. He didn't care which.

They reached the edge of one of the craters and turned along it, staying hidden in the jungle. He could smell the odor of death. He could feel it. Finally he turned and stepped out into the open.

And couldn't believe what greeted him.

Even several hours after the last bomb had fallen, the VC were still stunned. There were enemy soldiers all over the place. Dozens of them. Some were on the ground, rolling from side to side. Some were sitting with their backs against broken trees or piles of dirt that had been thrown up by the bombs. Some were staggering around in a daze. All of them were bleeding. Their faces were covered in blood and it stained their uniforms.

Connel stood still at the edge of the jungle for a moment, trying to figure out what was going on. The enemy had obviously been close to the bombs when they had gone off. Maybe they had been hiding in their tunnels, thinking that thirty feet of earth would protect them. Connel wondered how many were still buried under the rubble.

One of the enemy soldiers turned toward him and seemed to realize that he was there. The VC held his hands out, palms up, asking for help. He didn't know Connel was the enemy. Or if he did, he didn't care.

Connel raised his rifle, aimed but didn't fire. He stared into the blank face of the VC, looked into the man's brown eyes, blood caked under them like tear streaks, and felt a hatred he'd never known he possessed. Slowly he squeezed the trigger, and the round hit the VC in the chest, knocking him to the ground like a rag doll.

The shot had no effect on the others. It was as if they hadn't heard it, or having heard it, didn't recognize it as a threat. None of them moved, reacted, ran or even jumped. They sat there stupidly, blood running from their ears, eyes, noses and mouths, too stunned to know what was happening.

Connel aimed at another enemy and shot him. The Vietcong soldier rolled off the log and lay still. The remainder of the enemy soldiers, another two dozen or more, didn't react.

"Kill them," said Connel. "Shoot them."

He fired at another, wounding the man, who clamped a hand to his shoulder. Connel put another bullet into his head and the VC soldier died.

One of the strikers opened fire then. He shot two of the VC and then refused to shoot again. He stood quietly, his weapon held in his hands, watching the enemy.

Connel didn't notice. He was in a shooting gallery with real live targets that didn't move much. He aimed at one of the staggering figures and dropped him. He shot one near the rim of a crater and was delighted to see the man topple over, disappearing below.

Giggling, he kept firing. Single shots. He watched a head fly apart in a spray of crimson. He saw the body drop in a loose-boned way that told him the man was dead before he hit the ground. He shot the foot off another and then killed him with a shot in the chest.

Then, dropping the empty magazine from his rifle, he slammed another home and charged the weapon. At that moment he realized the strikers weren't shooting. They just stood there and watched.

"You think they wouldn't shoot you if the situation was reversed?" Connel asked them. "You think they care about the rules of war? They'd kill you just as quickly as they could, and you know it."

"We should take prisoners."

"Why?" demanded Connel. "What could they possibly tell us that we'd want to know? Just kill them. That's the way you win a war. You kill the enemy."

Connel opened fire again, pulling the trigger rapidly. He kept shooting and shooting, pouring more rifle fire into the clearing where the stunned soldiers were dying one by one. Connel kept shooting at them until they were all on the ground, all with bullets in them. Twenty of them. Twenty-five. In less than fifteen minutes he'd passed the number of men killed by Billy the Kid. Legend had it that Billy had killed twenty-one men before he was twenty-one. Connel had just killed twenty-five before he was twenty-five.

He emptied the magazine into the clearing and then reloaded. Satisfied, he stood up and moved toward the first body. He touched the dead man with his toe, then turned and looked back at his tiny patrol. "Get the weapons," he said, waving them forward.

But there wasn't much in the way of weapons. The VC, having fled from the tunnels, had lost their weapons. They had been too frightened to think of anything except escape.

The strikers moved out and walked over the field, checking the bodies. They gathered the little they could find of military value—some papers from one body, insignia from the uniform of another, and any weapons they could find.

Connel moved forward and found that one of the Vietcong was still alive. He had a sucking chest wound and his breath whistled laboriously. Connel looked back and saw that no one was watching him. The strikers were busy with their tasks.

He knelt near the VC, reached out with his right hand, clutched the man's neck and began to squeeze slowly. The VC didn't react at first. Then, as it became harder to breathe, he tensed and his muscles stiffened. But he didn't have the strength to fight back. Instead he gasped once and died.

Connel stood and turned. There was nothing left to do. It was time to get out and back up the slope. Up there to wait while Gerber and Suttin continued to observe. What would they think when they came to this place? Two dozen dead, shot. That would confuse them.

He glanced back at the field and then noticed something very strange. He was alone. The strikers had left him with the dead. Left him all alone.

16

IN THE JUNGLE NORTH
OF BANG RON

The firing drifted to them, barely audible in the distance. Gerber knew it was a single M-16. He moved to the RTO and grabbed the handset. "Headhunter Six, this is Zulu Six. Are you in contact?"

There was a moment of silence, then, "That's a negative, Zulu."

"Headhunter Five, this is Zulu Six."

Again he waited, but this time there was no answer. "Headhunter Five, say status."

Finally he was answered. "This is Headhunter Five."

Gerber knew the speaker wasn't Connel but one of the strikers. He keyed his own mike. "Say status."

There was a pause before the voice said, "We wait."

"Break, break. Headhunter Six. Did you copy?"

"Roger."

Gerber squeezed his eyes shut momentarily while he tried to figure out what was going on. One weapon firing didn't make an attack. Suttin hadn't reported any kind of contact. But someone was shooting. And where was Connel?

"Headhunter Six, this is Zulu Six. Let's pull out of here."

"Ah, roger, Zulu. I haven't completed the sweep."

"Roger, that. Let's get out, anyway. Meet you at the rendezvous point."

"Roger."

Gerber gave the handset back to the RTO. He found his senior NCO. "Let's get the men together and get the hell out of here. I want to be ready to move up to the top of the ridge in five minutes."

"Yes, sir." He raised his voice slightly and called to the others in Vietnamese.

Gerber moved down the valley slightly and then used his binoculars. There was nothing to see except more craters, broken trees and mounds of earth. Then the Vietnamese NCO approached. "We ready. Somebody come."

"Do you know who?"

"No. Quiet."

"Can you find your way to the blocking patrol on top of the ridge?"

"Yes, sir."

"Then take the point and move up the slope. Go for ten minutes, then stop. If you hear nothing, do it again and keep working uphill in cycles. If you hear shooting down here, stay where you are until I catch up with you."

"Yes, sir."

"Then go."

The NCO ran off and waved at the strikers. He hurried past them, hesitated at the very edge of the jungle, then vanished into the trees. Gerber turned and dropped to one knee. He scanned the jungle all around him but still could find no sign of the enemy.

Then, just as he was about to give up, he heard a noise, a quiet sound, barely perceptible. Gerber put the binoculars away and stood up. Facing the direction of the sound, he retreated toward the jungle.

There was a flash of movement in front of him, and he dropped to one knee and raised his rifle. A single enemy soldier appeared. His khaki uniform was torn and dirty. A moment later two more appeared. All of the VC looked as if they were slightly dazed, as if the bombing were still affecting them.

One of them looked at Gerber, then seemed to look through him. Slowly the man raised his weapon, as if to fire. Gerber shot once and the man fell backward. The other two reacted immediately. They split, running in opposite directions. The first man threw himself behind the wall of dirt that ringed one of the craters. The other ran into the jungle and disappeared. Gerber turned his attention to the second man. The VC fired once, but the bullet went wide. Gerber shot back, and the round kicked up some dirt. Then he fired again and the man dropped.

Gerber backed up toward the jungle, turned suddenly, then continued forward. There was no noise around him. Nothing. Satisfied that he was alone, he moved deeper into the trees.

A moment later he saw one of the strikers. They were coming back to help him. Gerber waved at them, telling them to turn and head up the slope.

SUTTIN, AFTER GETTING word from Gerber, didn't hesitate. He waved the men together and then ordered them up the slope. One of the NCOs took the point, and as the men left the moonscape, Suttin counted, making sure everyone was there. One of his men had discovered a broken, twisted AK and was carrying it. That was the only real sign of the enemy that Suttin or his men had seen in the past ten minutes.

They slipped into the jungle and picked their way up the slope rapidly. When the shooting started behind them, they all dived for cover. Suttin turned and looked, but couldn't see anything. He crawled toward the RTO, took the handset from the man and whispered "Zulu Six, Zulu Six, this is Headhunter Six."

There was no answer. He waited for thirty seconds, then repeated the message. But by then the firing had stopped. There had been only a few rounds exchanged. Suttin didn't know what it meant or what to do. Should he return to lend support, or continue toward the summit?

There was no more shooting, so Suttin decided there was no reason to return. Gerber had ordered him to get to the top of the ridge.

He gave the handset back to the RTO and then, keeping low, worked his way forward to the pointman. Leaning close, he said, "Let's get moving again."

The pointman nodded and stood. He moved into the jungle and was followed by the remainder of the patrol. Suttin waited and let the men pass him. When they were all clear, he fell in behind them.

They climbed the gentle slope rapidly, forcing their way through the vegetation. The pointman stopped once, crouched for a minute, then stood and continued the climb. As they approached the summit, they slowed, then halted. Suttin pushed his way forward to the front of the patrol. He found the pointman standing next to a palm tree. The man glanced back at Suttin. "We close now."

Suttin nodded. He stared into the jungle but couldn't see anything. Kneeling for a moment, he surveyed the trees and bushes, but there was nothing to see. Finally he stood and moved to the rear, where the RTO was waiting. Taking the handset, he said, "Headhunter Five, this is Six."

"Go."

"We're near your location and coming in."

"Ah, roger."

Suttin gave the handset back to the RTO, then looked at the man for a moment. Connel should have answered him, not one of the strikers. That worried him. Connel should have been close enough to the radio to answer calls.

He shrugged, turned and moved back toward the point. Crouching, he said, "We're going in now."

"Yes, sir," the NCO on point answered.

With that they pressed forward.

As GERBER CLIMBED the slope, he knew they were being followed. Whoever it was, they weren't stumbling around, but moving with careful military precision. It sounded as if there was a platoon, maybe as many as fifty men.

Gerber caught up with the rear of his patrol and pushed on past it. He came to the pointman, knelt near him and said, "Straight to the top now toward the reinforcements."

The NCO looked at him, his face bathed in sweat, his eyes big. "Hurry?"

"Slow and steady," said Gerber. "We don't want to give anything away. Go now."

Without a word, the man was up and moving. He pushed through the jungle, no longer worried about leaving any signs. It was obvious that the enemy knew where they were.

Gerber let the rest of the patrol pass him, then fell in behind. If the enemy had been pressing them closely, he would have hung back to lob a grenade or two at them, but that wasn't necessary. The VC hadn't gotten within two hundred yards. Gerber was certain of that.

They reached the top of the ridge, and the pointman didn't stop. He followed the crest, working his way east, and the patrol strung out behind him.

Gerber was going to call a momentary halt, but the pointman burst from cover and was standing among the other strikers. They had trained their weapons on him but hadn't fired, wanting to identify the target before killing it. Gerber followed the patrol in and then watched as his men filtered out, joining the perimeter established by Connel when he had taken the position.

"Connel's gone," said Suttin.

"What?"

"Connel took four men and headed down to the bombing area. The eastern end of it. The men with him have come back, but not Connel. Connel was the one doing the shooting we heard earlier."

"They tell you what happened to him?"

"They say he's dead."

"Bullshit!" Gerber snapped.

"You think they left him?"

"Hell, yes. They're getting even with him for leaving their comrades the day before."

"What are we going to do?" asked Suttin.

Before Gerber could answer, someone opened fire. One weapon on full-auto. Twenty quick rounds and then only the sounds of the echo through the jungle.

The strikers dived for cover. Gerber looked in the direction of the shooting, then began to crawl forward, his face only inches from the rotting vegetation on the jungle floor. He reached the perimeter and glanced right and left. There were strikers visible on either side of them, their weapons held ready.

Now Gerber was going to try to find out who had fired and why. He turned right and there was another burst, this one from in front of him. An AK shooting into the jungle.

Gerber dropped flat and let his thumb slide along his weapon to touch the safety. He made sure it was off as he watched the jungle in front of him.

A small man carrying an AK loomed out of the shadows. Gerber swung around to aim at him, but before he could fire, someone else let loose. A splash of crimson appeared on the man's chest near the shoulder. He whirled, dropped his weapon and fell into some bushes.

Firing erupted all at once then. Muzzle-flashes sparkled in the shadows of the jungle, marking the locations of the enemy. Two, three and then a dozen. Rounds snapped through the air overhead, slamming into the trees. Bark and bits of leaves rained down. Tracers, some bright, some pale, lanced through the jungle, a few tumbling upward into the canopy.

Gerber rolled to the right, pushing his shoulder against a tree. He searched for a target, found one and fired. There was an answering burst, the bullets thudding into the tree next to him. Gerber put three quick rounds into the muzzle-flash of the VC's weapon. The man stopped firing abruptly.

All around him the men were shooting faster and faster. The noise of individual weapons was lost in the hammering of all the others. Then a grenade exploded. The detonation rang in Gerber's ears.

Movement to the left caught his attention. He fired at it but missed. The Vietcong dived for cover and rolled. Gerber watched the man's progress in the vegetation. As the VC stopped and popped up, Gerber fired at him, but missed again.

The enemy fell back without shooting, but the bushes began to wave again. This time Gerber flipped to full-auto and put a burst into a bush. A high-pitched wail marked his success.

Now Chicom grenades began to detonate. One, two, three of them. Small, quiet pops accompanied by a brief rain of debris. It could only mean the VC were trying to disengage.

"Don't let them go!" yelled Gerber. He got to his feet, taking cover behind a tree.

One of the strikers was up, firing, then was suddenly hit. He flipped back and didn't move.

"Take them!" yelled Gerber.

There was movement to his right—black silk against the deep green of the jungle. Gerber fired at the center of it. A man appeared, an AK in his hand, firing from the hip. The rounds tore through the vegetation, but missed Gerber. The captain aimed carefully and dropped the man.

Just then the enemy firing tapered off. Gerber didn't want the VC to break contact, but he didn't think he had enough men to give chase. They could easily walk into an ambush where a hundred VC, two hundred, waited. When he was sure no AKs were firing and that all the rounds were outgoing, he yelled, "Cease fire! Cease fire! Cease fire!"

Slowly the M-16s fell silent. When the last of the echoes died away and the jungle was quiet, Gerber slipped to the rear. Suttin stood there, his face covered with dirt. He looked shocked.

"You okay?" asked Gerber.

"Yeah."

"What's our status here?"

"I'll have to check."

Gerber nodded. "Then get on it. And we'll have to see about getting out pronto."

"We finished?"

"I saw the bomb damage and I saw a little evidence that the VC have been hurt. You?"

"Bodies. Lots of them. And those strikers who went with Connel said they found a bunch of VC who had been stunned in the raid."

"That's good enough for me," said Gerber.

Suttin nodded and turned, moving deeper into the perimeter. Gerber started his own survey. He headed first to where he'd seen the striker fall. The man was dead, a bullet through his head. Moving to the left, he found another striker who had been killed, the round ripping open his stomach. Next to him was a survivor. Then two more. Gerber touched the shoulder of one of them and nodded toward the center of the perimeter. "Let's pull it in a little."

The men did as they were told. One of them dragged the body of a dead striker. Gerber told them to find the other man and pull his body back, too.

Suttin appeared then. "We've got seven dead and nine wounded. Two of those should be evacked as soon as possible, or they're going to die quickly."

"Can you get them to the camp?"

"I don't think so. We need to get them out."

"Coordinate that on the radio with Sergeant Fetterman. Chopper'll have to use a jungle penetrator."

"Why not take them down to the bombing zone? Chopper could land there."

"You'd have to make sure the zone's clear, and we know there are VC in the area."

"Yes, sir, but it's a lot closer and we don't have to fart around with the jungle penetrator."

"Okay," said Gerber slowly. "Besides, someone has to go down and look for Connel. I'll tag along with you and then break off. I'll take two of the strikers Connel had with him."

Suttin hesitated, then asked, "How's that going to look? Connel refuses to go back for strikers he left, but we go back to get him."

"It'll look bad," said Gerber, "but I'm not leaving anyone in the field until I know he's dead. That's the only way you can operate."

"The strikers are going to be pissed off."

"It'll be up to you to explain it to them. Make them realize that I would do the same for a striker if he was left behind. One of our soldiers is one of our soldiers. I'm not Connel and you're not Connel."

"Yes, sir."

Gerber was worried. It was getting late. Before long they would be stuck in the jungle overnight in an area infested with VC. "Get enough choppers to airlift us all out of here," he told Suttin. "With gun support."

Suttin grinned. "Yes, sir."

"And once you've done that, we'll get moving. I'll go and collect Connel."

Suttin shrugged and walked off toward the RTO. Gerber watched him and knew he was right. There was no easy way to explain to the strikers why he had to go after Connel when the lieutenant didn't go back after their comrades. That was going to be a problem. But right now the problem was Connel.

17

IN THE JUNGLE NORTH
OF BANG RON

Suttin arranged the air transport and the Medevac while Gerber talked to the men who had accompanied Connel into the valley. He selected two of them to go with him, along with one of the RTOs. Then he searched for Suttin.

"This is going to work perfectly," Gerber said when he found the lieutenant. "With you at one end and helicopters coming in as a diversion, I should be able to locate Connel."

"This isn't a good idea," said Suttin.

"I know," agreed Gerber, "but how would you feel if you were the one in the jungle with no help?"

"I understand that," said Suttin.

"Then let's get to it."

Suttin glanced at the center of the perimeter where the stretchers were being made. The bodies of the dead were wrapped in poncho liners and tied to long, slender poles to make it easier to get them down the slope. Everyone looked ready.

"Go," said Gerber.

Suttin moved to the north side of the perimeter, then with one man to cover him, moved out on point. Those with the dead and the stretchers filled in while the remainder brought up the rear.

Gerber watched the whole party move out. Then he stood and said, ''Let's go.''

Gerber, walking point, pushed into the jungle. He moved down the slope slowly, watching and listening, knowing the enemy was close. Methodically he checked over his shoulder, making sure the strikers were still there. He wouldn't have been surprised if they suddenly faded into the jungle.

After a few minutes, he stopped to listen, then continued on. Following the general path used by Connel, he searched the jungle around him, looking for booby traps and signs of the enemy. They reached the valley floor and halted again. Gerber surveyed the area but could only see trees, bushes, ferns and the carpet of dead vegetation. Once again he could smell the results of the B-52 strike. The bombs had so destroyed that section of the world that it would be years before the damage faded from sight, even in a tropical environment.

The shot came as a surprise. Gerber dropped, then cocked his head and listened. An M-16 had fired in the distance, maybe two hundred, three hundred yards away, though in the jungle it was sometimes hard to tell. He looked over his shoulder. The Vietnamese strikers were still there, holding their weapons at the ready.

Gerber got up and began to move forward. He was crouched now, like an old man fighting a breeze. His head swiveled as he searched the jungle around him.

There was no answering shot, nothing to suggest that the enemy was closing in on Connel or that he was fighting for his life. Gerber kept moving and eventually came to the edge of the jungle. A long line of craters was spread out in front of him.

The strikers joined him. He glanced at the men and then back out. He wanted to move along the edge of the jungle, just inside it where they would have some cover.

There was another shot and then a third. An AK fired back on full-auto, a short burst that ripped apart the silence of the jungle. Then, from the east, far to the east, came the beat of helicopter rotors. The pop of the blades was nearly lost in the distance, but they were there, coming closer.

Gerber was up and moving then, hurrying forward. There was more firing. A single M-16 against two, three, maybe four AKs. The enemy was moving in to get Connel. Kill the single man to make up for all their friends killed in the bombing and in the failed ambush.

He stopped as he approached the firefight. Crouched low, he worked his way forward, searching the jungle for the enemy. As he reached the edge of the jungle, he spotted Connel in a crater. The lieutenant was lying near the top of it, using it as a giant foxhole. Scattered around it were the bodies of the soldiers Connel had killed. Now he was firing into the jungle at the unseen enemy.

Gerber stood up and tried to see across the line of craters. He searched for the muzzle-flashes of the enemy weapons and looked for movement in the trees, but the only thing he could see was Connel shooting into the jungle.

"ROGER. We'll throw smoke," said Suttin. He nodded to a striker and the man tossed a grenade out. "Be advised that the ground is rough."

"Roger, rough. ID yellow."

"Roger, yellow. We're lined up in a staggered trail. Dead for the last chopper, wounded for the two in front of that."

"Roger. Inbound."

Suttin tossed the handset away and turned to the east, searching for the choppers. He didn't like standing in the open field with no strikers in the trees as flankers. They were vulnerable. The enemy could slip in and open fire, killing them before the choppers arrived. But Suttin wanted everyone on the choppers within thirty seconds of their arrival. Then he spotted the helicopters in the distance, low on the horizon, a cluster of black specks coming toward him, growing larger rapidly.

The cloud of yellow smoke drifted into the jungle on their right. Suttin pulled another grenade, made sure it was yellow, then threw it out. There was a quiet pop and more smoke began to float upward.

The strikers shifted around nervously. Suttin took a deep breath. He glanced at his weapon, at the safety, which was off, and then back at the helicopters, wondering why it was taking them so long to get there. It was as if an unseen hand were pushing them away.

"Someone comes," one of the strikers said suddenly.

"Where?"

"There."

Suttin turned, but couldn't see anything. He glanced back at the choppers and was amazed to see them begin to flare, exposing the undersides of their fuselages. One of them had a giant peace symbol painted on the bottom. Another said Here We Come.

"Get ready!" Suttin yelled.

The rotor wash hit him, and he staggered. The noise of the turbines was overwhelming as dust flew up and choked him. As the skids touched the ground, Suttin ordered, "Get going! Get going!"

He took a step toward the lead chopper, his eyes fixed on the rear where the strikers were struggling to get the stretchers and dead loaded. Then there was a ripping noise behind him—a single machine gun firing.

The door guns on one chopper opened up. The muzzle-flash strobed, a tube of fire three feet long. Red tracers danced into the jungle as more enemy soldiers opened fire. Suttin heard the snap of the rounds as they punched through the thin skin of the tail boom.

Whirling, he saw the jungle alive with fireflies. A dozen, two dozen, a hundred weapons shooting. And then the jungle blew up. Rockets fired by the gunships began to rain down in pairs, and balls of orange fire exploded among the trees.

The second gunship rolled in, miniguns blazing. It looked as if the sides of the chopper were on fire. Red tracers danced through the jungle, tearing it to shreds. The enemy soldiers fired through the canopy at the choppers. But that didn't stop them. The third gunship rolled in and let loose with its grenade launcher, and 40 mm grenades tore into the trees, ripping the VC to pieces.

Suttin saw that everyone was on board. He ran to the skid of the lead chopper and climbed up. As his feet touched it, the chopper lifted, hovered momentarily, then took off, the door guns pouring a steady stream of 7.62 mm rounds into the jungle. Ten machine guns raked the trees as the gunships continued their runs, trying to suppress the enemy activity.

They stayed low for a few moments, using the canopy of the jungle for cover as they climbed the ridge. But once they were over the top, they began a rapid climb out.

Suttin slipped closer to the hatch and looked back into the jungle. The gunships still worked there, hammering away at the trees. Some tracers, a pale green, flashed upward. But that was nothing compared to what was pouring down. Rockets, grenades and machine-gun fire slashed at the enemy.

At that moment Suttin touched the pilot on the shoulder and shouted, "I've got four, five people left down there."

"The hell you say."

"Will you be able to get them out?"

"Shit, I don't know."

GERBER WATCHED the choppers fly over. One or two of the enemy soldiers fired up at them, but with no effect whatsoever. Connel kept a steady stream of fire into the jungle opposite them.

Gerber heard the choppers land. When he was sure Connel could hear him, he shouted, "Can you get out of there?"

Connel didn't seem to notice. He was concentrating on firing at the enemy.

"Can you get out of there?" Gerber yelled again.

This time Connel glanced back. Then, with his attention on the jungle, he shouted, "I'm pinned down!"

"We'll cover," said Gerber. "You'll have to get yourself out."

Connel kept firing until his weapon was empty. Then he slipped farther down the side of the crater and worked at reloading his M-16, tossing away the empty magazine. "Ready," he yelled.

Gerber had tried to spot the enemy but couldn't see them. They were concealed in the jungle and had stopped shooting. Maybe they were waiting for a chance at the helicopters, though Gerber knew they wouldn't be back, or maybe they were afraid of the gunships.

Gerber ordered the strikers to spread out. "On my command, open fire. Dump everything into the woods as fast as you can fire, but don't use full-auto. Single shot. Understand?"

The men nodded. They fanned out and crouched behind the available cover. Gerber checked his own weapon and then shouted, "We're getting ready." He couldn't see Connel and assumed the man had moved around to be in a better position to get out of the crater.

"Fire!" yelled Gerber, pulling the trigger of his own weapon.

As Connel fired, he scrambled over the lip of the crater and sprawled on the ground. Leaping suddenly, he sprinted toward the cover of the jungle, dodging right and left, until he reached Gerber and his men.

Gerber emptied his weapon and hit the release. He jerked a magazine from his bandolier, slammed it home, worked the bolt, then fired three quick shots. But Connel had reached the safety of the trees, diving through the wall of vegetation like a base runner in a headfirst slide.

"You okay?" yelled Gerber.

"I'm fine. Let's get the hell out of here."

But Gerber didn't stop firing. He kept pouring rounds into the jungle on the other side of the bomb line. If they broke contact immediately, they'd have a three- or four-hundred-yard head start. If the enemy hesitated at all, they could be a klick or more ahead of them before the VC realized they had gotten out.

Gerber emptied his weapon and dropped to the ground, his back against a tree. He listened to the AKs firing across the open area at them. Then he glanced over and saw Connel crawling toward him.

Gerber reloaded quickly. He waited until Connel was close, then whispered, "We've got to get out of here."

"I'm ready."

"Head on up the slope but stop. We'll break contact."

"Yes, sir."

Gerber stood up but kept his back to the tree. He closed his eyes for an instant, then took a breath, then whirled around and fired five quick shots. "Go!" he told Connel.

The younger man leaped to his feet but kept his head down. He hurried into the jungle and ran up the slope.

Gerber glanced to the right and said, "Let's get moving. Disengage."

The closest striker looked at him, understood and then gave the order in quiet Vietnamese. The firing tapered slightly.

"Go," said Gerber, and the man closest turned to run. One by one the strikers stopped shooting and headed back up the slope, the line stringing out over fifty yards. Only Gerber was left at the edge of the jungle.

He stopped firing and waited. Slowly, one at a time, the VC opposite him stopped shooting, too. He knew what would happen next. The enemy would begin to filter out of the trees, working their way toward him. When they did, he'd fire a few rounds, force them back, and then he'd get out.

The first VC appeared a moment later. He showed himself and then dived back into the cover of the jungle. Gerber waited, and another enemy tried to draw fire.

He jumped out, stood for a moment and then disappeared. When there was no shooting, a couple of them came out and began to work their way across the bomb field, using the overturned earth and the bodies of the dead for protection.

Gerber aimed at the closest man, let him stand up and then fired. The round caught him in the center of the chest and threw him back. He flopped to the ground, his hands and feet drumming in the dirt as he wailed in pain, the screams getting higher and higher until they suddenly stopped.

Gerber watched the second soldier flee. Firing erupted along the jungle line opposite, but the rounds were poorly aimed. Now it was time for him to get out. He turned and ran straight back and up the slope. Stopping once, he listened, but the enemy firing didn't taper off. They'd keep firing for another five or ten minutes and then, realizing that no one was shooting back, stop. They'd wait longer before trying to explore, or they'd take the long way around trying to flank him. Either way gave him all the time he needed.

He hurried up the slope, slipped once on the soft, wet ground and fell to one knee. But that didn't slow him much. He leaped up and ran, climbing toward the summit. In front of him he saw the back of one of the strikers.

"Right behind you," said Gerber, so that the striker wouldn't be surprised by someone suddenly catching up to him.

Together they finished the climb. They found Connel, the other striker and the RTO sitting on the ground, all breathing hard. Neither of the strikers looked up as Gerber and the last man came in. Connel was standing, leaning against the trunk of a palm, his rifle pointed at the two Vietnamese with him.

"Bastards left me," he said, wheezing.

"They came back," said Gerber.

"They left me there to get picked off by the VC. The bastards deserve to die."

"Lieutenant," said Gerber, "we have enough problems now. We have to get out of here or we'll all die."

Connel glanced at Gerber and then at the two men sitting on the ground. He ignored the third man who was close to Gerber and who had turned his rifle toward Connel. He'd forgotten all about the third striker.

There wasn't time to argue. Gerber could still hear firing from the VC, but it was sporadic. They were beginning to figure out the situation and in a few minutes would be running across the field. Gerber stepped between Connel and the strikers, turning his back on them. He knew that it was a risk, but there was no other way to handle the problem. "Take the point," he told Connel.

"I don't want these guys behind me."

"Take the point, now," said Gerber. He stared at the younger man. "Take it or I'll shoot you."

Connel hesitated, then glanced out into the jungle. He raised the barrel of his weapon so that it was pointing up at the canopy. "Okay."

"Go," said Gerber. "I'll watch these guys. Go."

Connel turned suddenly and was gone. Gerber motioned the others to their feet. "We've got to move it."

They hurried off the summit of the ridge. As Gerber moved, he heard the last of the firing die away. The VC had finally realized that no one was shooting back at them.

Gerber and his men ran down the hill and through the jungle, heading for the camp. They leaped a narrow stream that was nearly dry, ran around an outcropping of rock and raced for the edge of the jungle. Gerber was no longer worried about finesse. Now it was time to put distance between themselves and the enemy.

He felt the first pain in his throat. Then it was deep in his chest, radiating upward and outward. He felt it grow until he was sure it would kill him. And even with that, with his arms and legs suddenly leaden, he kept running. When he came to a log, he didn't have the strength left to hurdle it. Instead he jumped on top of it and then leaped off.

Behind him he heard noises. The enemy was gaining on him. He couldn't understand that. They should have taken an hour to climb the hill. Maybe they had run the whole way. Maybe the shooting had been a diversion. Or maybe some of the VC had flanked his position quickly and had run up the slope while he and Connel had argued.

He thought about stopping so he could put a burst into his pursuers. Then he thought about his grenades. Instead he decided to keep running.

And then, suddenly, the jungle thinned, and in the half-light of the onrushing dusk, he saw the edge of the killing zone. As he got closer, he saw Connel out in the knee-high elephant grass, running, zigzagging, as he headed for the camp. A moment later the first of the Vietnamese strikers appeared. The RTO came out, but he no longer had the radio. Somewhere back there he'd thrown it away.

Gerber burst from the cover of the jungle, now convinced that the VC weren't more than fifty or sixty yards behind him. He'd never make it to the camp in time. He'd be caught in the open, far from safety.

But then Fetterman was standing there in front of him. Fetterman and a skirmish line. Fetterman and fifty men, all armed, their weapons pointed at the jungle.

"Hit the dirt, Captain!" ordered the master sergeant.

As Gerber hit the ground, the skirmishers opened fire. A wall of lead flew toward the jungle, and the VC were caught by surprise.

18

BANG RON

Gerber sat at the table, drinking a cold Coke. Connel and Suttin nursed cold beers opposite him, while Fetterman stood close to the door. Gerber was tired, more than he should have been. It might have been a result of Connel's attitude in the field, or his attitude toward the Vietnamese. Whatever it was, the added pressure had taken a lot out of him.

Fetterman, looking fresh and clean, moved forward, then sat down. "I think everything's in place now. We shouldn't be disturbed."

"Have you got the guards out?" asked Suttin.

"Man in the fire control tower, men in the corner bunkers and more scattered throughout the line."

"You expecting trouble?" asked Connel. He lifted the beer and drank deeply.

"I always expect trouble," said Fetterman.

Connel wiped the back of his hand over his mouth, then leaned forward. "So what are we going to talk about?"

Gerber stared at the younger officer. "How about that little scene in the jungle? The Vietcong are threatening us and you try to get into a firefight with our strikers."

"Bastards ran off and left me to die," said Connel. "Fuckers aren't worth the powder it would take to blow them all up."

"Those fuckers saved my butt more than once," said Fetterman.

Connel glanced at Fetterman, saw the look in his eyes and knew enough to back off.

"Tell me what happened," said Gerber.

"Okay," said Connel. "Okay." He blinked and leaned closer to Gerber, as if planning a conspiracy with the captain. "I was on the ridge with the blocking force, the reinforcements."

"And you left your post," said Gerber.

"No, sir. I left the main force there, right where they had to be, but I got to thinking that the enemy could filter down the line. If that happened, they might escape. I figured me and a couple of others could slow them down, maybe turn them, if we were in the right place."

"Those weren't your orders," said Gerber.

Connel shook his head as if he hadn't heard the words or didn't understand them. He pressed on. "I selected the men to go with me and we slipped down the slope to the edge of the bomb line. When we got there, we found dozens of VC milling around. They were just standing there as if they didn't know what was happening."

"Shock from the bombing?" asked Fetterman.

Connel shrugged. "Hell, I don't know." He picked up his beer, drank some, then set the can down again. "Anyway, we wanted to check for papers, pick up the rifles, that sort of thing. We were doing it, too, and then

I looked around and the strikers were gone. They ran off and left me alone.''

"No reason for it?" asked Gerber.

"None that I could see, sir. One minute they were there and the next they were gone. They didn't say a word and they didn't make any noise."

"What did you do?" asked Suttin.

"I thought about running off after them but, hell, I wasn't in any danger. I figured I'd finish the search. That's what I was doing when there were some shots from the jungle. I dived into a crater for protection. I was doing fine when help arrived."

"So," said Gerber, "when you got up the hill, you thought you'd shoot a couple of the people who rescued you."

"They didn't rescue me," said Connel. "You did. If it hadn't been for you, I'd still be there."

Suttin looked at Connel. "You must have said or done something. They wouldn't just run off."

"That's what they did."

"You must have done something," pressed Fetterman.

"No," said Connel.

Gerber interrupted. "There's one thing I don't understand. You said there were VC around the field. Stunned. What happened to them?"

"I shot them." Connel grinned. "They were out of it. They didn't have a clue about what was going on. The strikers didn't shoot much, but we killed them just the same."

Fetterman slammed the table with his hand. "Jesus Christ."

"What are you getting so upset about?" asked Connel. "They were the enemy."

"You don't murder helpless people," said Fetterman.

"That's a damn funny idea from a soldier," countered Connel.

Fetterman lowered his voice. There was a knifelike edge to it. "I'm a soldier, not a murderer."

"But they were VC. If I didn't kill them when I did, they'd soon get well and start killing Americans."

"No," said Gerber. "There are prohibitions against shooting the wounded. If they were as stunned as you say, they could have been taken prisoner. There was no reason to shoot them." Gerber felt the rage boil through him. "Don't you understand what you've done? That wasn't the act of a soldier. It was the act of a killer. You've made everything the American press writes about us true. We're supposed to be superior, compassionate, intelligent, but you've made us common killers."

"They're the enemy," said Connel.

"Shit," said Fetterman.

"How many did you shoot?" asked Gerber.

"I don't know. Ten or twelve."

"The strikers saw that?" asked Gerber.

"Yes, sir."

"There's your answer, Captain," said Fetterman. "They got out when he killed those men."

"Couple that to his abandoning the strikers," said Suttin, "and we have the whole picture."

"That's not fair," said Connel.

Gerber raked a hand through his hair. He looked at Fetterman. "This gets out and there'll be an investigation. People will go to LBJ."

"You suggesting we bury it?" questioned Fetterman.

"I don't know," said Gerber. He stared at Connel. "You dumb son of a bitch."

"They were enemy soldiers. Armed enemy soldiers."

"That might be the one fact that saves you," said Gerber. "The only fact. If they had been Vietnamese civilians, just male civilians of a military age, you'd be up on charges right now. No question about it."

Fetterman looked hard at Gerber, but didn't say a word.

"You know, Connel," said Gerber, "we should file those charges...."

"You can't prove a thing."

Gerber laughed. "Let me ask you a question. Suppose I went to any of the Vietnamese strikers and told them what you did. Do you think they'd support you? Do you think you've earned their respect?"

"Fuck 'em," said Connel.

"And that's the other problem," said Gerber. "You don't like them and they don't like you. That's the real reason they left you. They had a chance and they took it. They watched you gun down helpless men and then ran off."

"Captain," said Fetterman, "what are we going to do?"

"I don't know." He fell silent, thinking. There was such a thing as loyalty to the soldiers. Connel seemed to believe that he had the right, the duty, to kill the enemy. That idea was beaten into the heads of recruits in basic training. The enemy was bad and deserved to be killed. Kill the enemy as quickly as possible. No one bothered to tell those impressionable soldiers that there were times when the enemy shouldn't be killed. There were times when the enemy should be captured.

Connel, according to his own words, had shot down helpless enemy soldiers. But then Gerber wondered why Connel's act was wrong if the bombing wasn't. The VC had been powerless to stop the bombs. The bombs had killed them at random. They could have killed civilians just as easily. Connel had been specific in his targets. Just enemy soldiers. How could the pilots, bombardiers and navigators be innocent of a war crime and Connel, who had shot enemy soldiers, be guilty?

"What are you going to do?" asked Connel, looking right at Gerber.

Suddenly the Coke wasn't strong enough. He wanted something with a little bite to it. These were the kind of decisions generals were paid to make. A captain wasn't supposed to make them.

"There's a specific policy on the commission of war crimes," said Suttin.

"I'm aware of the various regulations," said Gerber. "And I'm aware of the various shadings of those regulations."

"I would think—" began Connel.

"I'm not much interested in what you think," snapped Gerber.

"Captain," said Fetterman, "there's an old saying that a crime didn't take place if no one knows about it."

"You suggesting we just forget about this?"

"What can we do? Lieutenant Connel killed enemy soldiers, ones that Air Force officers had tried to kill a couple of hours earlier. No civilians were involved. And he's right about one thing. If we don't kill them now, they might end up killing us later."

Gerber shook his head.

"There was a submarine officer in World War II who machine-gunned Japanese soldiers in the water," Connel said.

"We're not talking about World War II."

"How can killing the enemy be considered wrong?" asked Connel.

And that was the real question. Connel had done his duty. He'd shot enemy soldiers. Men had received medals for doing it. Men had been promoted for doing it. Hell, men had become the President of the United States for doing it well. Killing the enemy was what war was all about.

Gerber made a decision suddenly, rapidly. He looked at Suttin. "You've got to get him out of here. Tonight. Back to Saigon for reassignment."

"Of course," said Suttin.

"And then we've got to forget about this. If anyone asks, he was pulled out because he couldn't work with the strikers. Hell, we can document that."

"It's not fair," said Connel.

"Shit," said Gerber. "It's more than fair. You have a problem, you go to the IG. Tell him what happened. I'll testify at your trial."

Fetterman looked at the men at the table. "Sometimes I don't understand this war."

Gerber nodded. "Sometimes I don't understand anything at all."

THE RESTAURANT WAS nearly empty, but then it was early to be eating dinner. The majority of the diners wouldn't be arriving for another two hours, but Gerber didn't care, not after everything that had happened in the past twenty-four hours.

He'd skipped eating so that he could debrief with Maxwell, telling him what the valley had looked like after a single B-52 raid. He'd told Maxwell about the Vietcong soldiers standing around, stunned by the bombing. He'd talked about the destruction he'd seen and that it looked as if the enemy was going to get out.

"How about another raid in there?" Maxwell had asked.

"Why not?" Gerber had said. "Anything that might have been missed the first time could be taken out now." And although he hadn't said it, he'd thought about the soldiers Connel had shot. Another raid would destroy the evidence. As Fetterman had said, if no one knew about it, then it didn't happen.

Maxwell had been satisfied with the report. He was convinced the B-52s had destroyed the VC power base. There would be no assault on Saigon soon. The enemy no longer had the people to do it. He'd told Gerber to go and get himself something to eat, then take some time off.

Now, sitting with him at the restaurant table, were Fetterman and Morrow. Both Gerber and Fetterman were wearing clean jungle fatigues. Morrow was dressed in her standard work uniform—an old flight suit with the arms hacked off at the elbows and the legs cut off above the knees. She hadn't taken time to change or shower but had hurried to the restaurant when Gerber had called.

"So where's this Connel now?" she asked.

"At the Ninetieth Replacement Battalion," said Gerber. "They'll probably send him up-country somewhere. Maybe all the way to I Corps to keep him out of everyone's hair."

She looked at Gerber. "I guess what I don't understand is your reluctance to prosecute the guy. Seems to me he was in violation of the regulations and should have been brought up on charges.''

''That was my first reaction,'' said Gerber. ''Man violates the law and he goes to jail, even if the law is rather idiotic. There's also something to be said for the idea that war is war.''

Morrow took a deep breath and looked squarely at Gerber. ''I've known you for a long time. I respect what you do. I don't always agree with it, and I'm not convinced we should be in Vietnam, but I respect you. But this time I just don't know.''

''What would you do?'' Fetterman asked her.

''Call the cops, so to speak. He murdered those people.''

''Then what do you do with the pilots dropping bombs in North Vietnam?'' Gerber asked. ''Whether anyone will admit it or not, they're killing civilians. They don't mean to, but it's happening.''

''But—'' she began.

''All Connel did was shoot men that we'd tried to blow up earlier. Why is it right to drop bombs on them but not shoot them thirty minutes later?''

''It's not the same thing,'' she said.

''But it is,'' Gerber insisted.

''The problem,'' Fetterman said, ''is that it's not a black-and-white issue. It's so damn gray that it's nearly impossible to resolve.''

''Your path is clear,'' Morrow told Gerber. ''Regulations spell out what you have to do.''

''Those regulations were written by men who have never been in combat. By men whose whole lives have been dedicated to politics.''

''Then I have no answer for you.''

Gerber nodded. "What you're saying is that I have to do what I think is right."

"Exactly."

For a moment Gerber sat silently while all the arguments circulated in his head. It was so clear and yet so obscure. Connel had only been fighting the war the best way he could. In some respects he was a hero. In others he wasn't. It all hinged on the timing. Shoot the VC before the bombs fell and he was a hero. Waiting until after they fell made him a murderer.

"Well?" Fetterman asked.

"There's only one thing we can do," Gerber said. "Eat."

"Is that all you're going to say?" Morrow asked.

Again Gerber hesitated. Then, knowing he was dodging the question, that he would always be haunted by his decision concerning Connel, he said, "Yes. That's it."

EPILOGUE

CHIEU HOI CLUB
PLEIKU

Lieutenant Marcus Connel sat with his back against the rough plywood wall and listened to the pounding beat of rock and roll pouring from the jukebox. Two women, American nurses who had braved the gauntlet of horny soldiers, were dancing with the two helicopter pilots who had brought them. The rest of the men stood around in a large, loose circle, watching the women dance. Connel wasn't interested in that.

All he cared about was the beer in front of him that was now lukewarm. It had been ice-cold when he had gotten it. It had been so cold that it had threatened to crack his teeth and freeze his eyeballs. But that had been thirty minutes earlier, and now it was nearly room temperature, which had to be pushing ninety.

Connel didn't like being at Pleiku. He didn't like being surrounded by so many Vietnamese. Not just members of the ARVN, but civilian workers allowed in each day to do the jobs the military didn't want to do or didn't have the time to do. He didn't like being banished so quickly from his first assignment.

But that was the important thing. He didn't *like* them. He hated almost nothing. He had matured in the past few weeks.

And as he drank his warm beer, he remembered the conversation he'd had so many months before. A college discussion on the war and how to run it. A dialogue among those who had yet to see combat. In that earlier discussion everything had been black and white. A soldier killed the enemy. Period. No quarter asked and none given.

Now, after his first brief tour in a combat environment, he understood the issue a little better. He understood what it was to take a human life. And even though he had killed a lot of men in the turkey shoot at the bomb site, he realized he had been wrong. He shouldn't have done it.

He knew that now. He regretted that it had happened, but he had learned from it. If the situation ever arose again, he would act differently. He was certain of that.

Finally he understood the nature of war. He understood what it meant to be a warrior. Understood it completely.

GLOSSARY

AC—Aircraft commander. The pilot in charge of the aircraft.

ADO—A-Detachment's area of operations.

AFVN—Armed Forces radio and television network in Vietnam. Army PFC Pat Sajak was probably the most memorable of AFVN's DJs with his loud and long, "GOOOOOOOOOOOOOD MORNing Vietnam!" The spinning Wheel of Fortune indicates that he makes his daily bread on late-night TV nowadays.

AGGRESSOR FATIGUES—Black fatigues so called because they are the color of the uniforms worn by the aggressors during war games in the World during training.

AIT—Advanced Individual Training. The school soldiers were sent to after basic.

AK-47—Assault rifle normally used by the North Vietnamese and Vietcong.

ANGRY-109—AN-109, the radio used by the Special Forces for long-range communications.

AN/PRR9 and AN/PRT4—An intrasquad radio receiver and transmitter used for short-range communications. The range is something under a mile.

AO—Area of Operations.

AO DAI—Long dresslike garment, split up the sides and worn over pants.

AP—Air Police. The old designation for the guards on Air Force bases. Now referred to as security police.

AP ROUNDS—Armor-piercing ammunition.

APU—Auxiliary Power Unit. An outside source of power used to start aircraft engines.

ARC LIGHT—Term used for a B-52 bombing mission. Also known as heavy arty.

ARVN—Army of the Republic of Vietnam. A South Vietnamese soldier. Also known as Marvin Arvin.

ASA—Army Security Agency.

ASH AND TRASH—Refers to helicopter support missions that didn't involve a direct combat role. They hauled supplies, equipment, mail and all sorts of ash and trash.

AST—Control officer between the men in isolation and the outside world. Responsible for taking care of all problems.

AUTOVON—Army phone system that allows soldiers on one base to call another base, bypassing the civilian phone system.

BDA—Bomb Damage Assessment. The official report on how well a bombing mission went.

BISCUIT—C-rations.

BODY COUNT—Number of enemy killed, wounded or captured during an operation. Used by Saigon and Washington as a means of measuring progress of the war.

BOOM BOOM—Term used by Vietnamese prostitutes to sell their product.

BOONDOGGLE—Any military operation that hasn't been completely thought out. A ridiculous operation.

BOONIE HAT—Soft Cap worn by a grunt in the field when not wearing his steel pot.

BROWNING M-2—Fifty-caliber machine gun manufactured by Browning.

BROWNING M-35—A 9 mm automatic pistol that became the favorite of the Special Forces.

BUSHMASTER—Jungle warfare expert or soldier skilled in jungle navigation. Also a large deadly snake not common to Vietnam but mighty tasty.

C AND C—Command and Control aircraft that circled overhead to direct combined air and ground operations.

CAO BOI—Cowboy. A term that referred to the criminals of Saigon who rode motorcycles.

CARIBOU—Cargo transport plane.

CHECKRIDE—Flight in which pilot checks the proficiency of another. It can be an informal review of the various techniques or a very formal test of a pilot's knowledge.

CHINOOK—Army Aviation twin-engine helicopter. A CH-47. Also known as a shit hook.

CHOCK—Refers to the number of the aircraft in the flight. Chock Three is the third. Chock Six is the sixth.

CLAYMORE—Antipersonnel mine that fires seven hundred and fifty steel balls with a lethal range of fifty meters.

CLOSE AIR SUPPORT—Use of airplanes and helicopters to fire on enemy units near friendlies.

CO CONG—Female Vietcong.

COLT—Soviet-built small transport plane. The NATO code name for Soviet and Warsaw Pact transports all begin with the letter *C*.

CONEX—Steel container about ten feet high, ten feet deep and ten feet long used to haul equipment and supplies.

CS—A chemical similar to tear gas used in Vietnam.

DAI UY—Vietnamese army rank equivalent to captain.

DEROS—Date Estimated Return from Overseas Service.

DIRNSA—Director, National Security Agency.

E AND E—Escape and Evasion.

FEET WET—Term used by pilots to describe flight over water.

FIELD GRADE—Refers to officers above the rank of captain and below that of brigadier general.

FIRECRACKER—Special artillery shell that explodes into a number of small bomblets that detonate later. The artillery version of the cluster bomb, it was a secret weapon employed tactically for the first time at Khe Sanh.

FIREFLY—Helicopter with a battery of bright lights mounted in or on it. The aircraft was designed to draw enemy fire at night so that gunships orbiting close by could attack the target.

FIRST SHIRT—Military term referring to the first sergeant.

FIVE—Radio call sign for the executive officer of a unit.

FNG—Fucking New Guy.

FOB—Forward Operating Base.

FOX MIKE—FM radio.

FREEDOM BIRD—Name given to any aircraft that took troops out of Vietnam. Usually referred to the commercial jet flights that took men back to the World.

GARAND—M-1 rifle that was replaced by the M-14. Issued to the South Vietnamese early in the war.

GO-TO-HELL RAG—Towel or any large cloth worn around the neck by a grunt.

GRAIL—NATO name for the shoulder-fired SA-7 surface-to-air missile.

GUARD THE RADIO—Term that means standing by in the commo bunker and listening for messages.

GUIDELINE—NATO name for the SA-2 surface-to-air missile.

GUNSHIP—Armed helicopter or cargo plane that carries weapons instead of cargo.

HE—High-explosive ammunition.

HOOTCH—Almost any shelter, from temporary to long-term.

HORN—Term that referred to a specific kind of radio operations that used satellites to rebroadcast messages.

HORSE—See *Biscuit*.

HOTEL THREE—Helicopter landing area at Saigon's Tan Son Nhut Airport.

HUEY—UH-1 helicopter.

HUMINT—Human intelligence resource.

ICS—Official name of the intercom system in an aircraft.

IG—Inspector General. The man appointed to make sure that each soldier is getting a fair deal. He fields the complaints of soldiers and watches for violations of the various military rules and regulations.

IN-COUNTRY—Term used to refer to American troops operating in South Vietnam. They were all in-country.

INTELLIGENCE—Any information about enemy operations. It can include troop movements, weapons capabilities, biographies of enemy commanders and general information about terrain features. Any information that can be useful in planning a mission.

KA-BAR—Type of military combat knife.

KIA—Killed In Action. (Since the U.S. wasn't engaged in a declared war, the use of the term KIA wasn't authorized. KIA came to mean enemy dead. Americans were KHA or Killed in Hostile Action.)

KLICK—A thousand meters. A kilometer.

LIMA LIMA—Land Line. Refers to telephone communications between two points on the ground.

LLDB—Luc Luong Dac Biet. The South Vietnamese Special Forces. Sometimes referred to as the Look Long, Duck Back.

LOW QUARTERS—Military term for regular shoes. In the case of the Army, it means the black dress shoes worn with Class A and dress uniforms.

LP—Listening Post. A position outside the perimeter manned by a couple of people to give advance warning of enemy activity.

LRRP—Long-Range Reconnaissance Patrol.

LSA—Lubricant used by soldiers on their weapons to ensure they will continue to operate properly.

LZ—Landing Zone.

M-3—Also known as a grease gun. A .45-caliber submachine gun favored in World War II by GIs. Its slow rate of fire meant the barrel didn't rise. As well, the user didn't burn through his ammo as fast as he did with some of his other weapons.

M-14—Standard rifle of the U.S., eventually replaced by the M-16. It fires the standard NATO round— 7.62 mm.

M-16—Became the standard infantry weapon of the Vietnam War. It fires the 5.56 mm ammunition.

M-79—Short-barreled, shoulder-fired weapon that fires a 40 mm grenade. These can be high explosives, white phosphorus or canister.

M-113—Numerical designation of an armored personnel carrier.

MACV—Military Assistance Command, Vietnam, replaced MAAG in 1964.

MAD MINUTE—Specified time on a base when the men in the bunkers would clear their weapons. It came to mean the random firing of all the camp's weapons just as fast as everyone could shoot.

MATCU—Marine Air Traffic Control Unit.

MEDEVAC—Also called Dust-Off. A helicopter used to take wounded to medical facilities.

MI—Military Intelligence.

MIA—Missing In Action.

MOS—Military Occupation Specialty.

MPC—Military Payment Certificates. Used by the military in lieu of U.S. dollars.

NCO—Noncommissioned officer. A noncom. A sergeant.

NCOIC—NCO In Charge. The senior NCO in a unit, detachment or patrol.

NDB—Nondirectional beacon. A radio beacon that can be used for homing.

NEXT—The man whose turn it was to be rotated home next. See *Short*.

NINETEEN—Average age of combat soldier in Vietnam, as opposed to twenty-six in World War II.

NVA—North Vietnamese Army. Also used to designate a soldier from North Vietnam.

ONTOS—Marine weapon that consists of six 106 mm recoilless rifles mounted on a tracked vehicle.

ORDER OF BATTLE—A listing of the units available during a battle. Not necessarily a list of how or when the units will be used, but a listing of who and what could be used.

P (PIASTER)—Basic monetary unit in South Vietnam worth slightly less than a penny.

PETA-PRIME—Tarlike substance that melted in the heat of the day to become a sticky black nightmare that clung to boots, clothes and equipment. It was used to hold down dust during the dry season.

PETER PILOT—Copilot in a helicopter.

PLF—Parachute Landing Fall. The roll used by parachutists on landing.

POL—Petroleum, Oil and Lubricants. The refueling point on many military bases.

POW—Prisoner of War.

PRC-10—Portable radio.

PRC-25—Lighter portable radio that replaced the PRC-10.

PULL PITCH—Term used by helicopter pilots that means they are going to take off.

PUNJI STAKE—Sharpened bamboo hidden to penetrate the foot. Sometimes dipped in feces.

PUZZLE PALACE—Term referring to the Pentagon. It was called the puzzle palace because no one knew what was going on in it. The Puzzle Palace East referred to MACV or USARV Headquarters in Saigon.

REDLEGS—Term that refers to artillerymen. It comes from the old Army where artillerymen wore red stripes on the legs of their uniforms.

RINGKNOCKER—Graduate of a military academy. The term refers to the ring worn by all graduates.

RON—Remain Over Night. Term used by flight crews to indicate a flight that lasted longer than a day.

RPD—Soviet 7.62 mm light machine gun.

RTO—Radio Telephone Operator. The radioman of a unit.

RUFF-PUFFS—Term applied to the RF-PFs, the regional forces and popular forces. Militia drawn from the local population.

S-3—Company-level operations officer. The same as the G-3 on a general's staff.

SA-2—Surface-to-air missile fired from a fixed site. Radar-guided, it is nearly thirty-five feet long.

SA-7—Surface-to-air missile that is shoulder-fired and has infrared homing.

SACSA—Special Assistant for Counterinsurgency and Special Activities.

SAFE AREA—Selected Area For Evasion. It doesn't mean that the area is safe from the enemy, only that the terrain, location or local population make the area a good place for escape and evasion.

SAM TWO—Refers to the SA-2 Guideline.

SAR—Search And Rescue forces.

SECDEF—Secretary of Defense.

SHORT-TIME—GI term for a quickie.

SHORT-TIMER—Person who had been in Vietnam for nearly a year and who would be rotated back to the World soon. When the DEROS (Date of Estimated Return from Overseas Service) was the shortest in the unit, the person was said to be next.

SINGLE-DIGIT MIDGET—Soldier with fewer than ten days left in-country.

SIX—Radio call sign for the unit commander.

SKATE—Term similar to gold-bricking.

SKS—Soviet-made carbine.

SMG—Submachine gun.

SOI—Signal Operating Instructions. The booklet that contained the call signs and radio frequencies of the units in Vietnam.

SOP—Standard Operating Procedure.

SPIKE TEAM—Special Forces team made up for a direct-action mission.

STEEL POT—Standard U.S. Army helmet. The steel pot was the outer metal cover.

TAOR—Tactical Area of Operational Responsibility.

TEAM UNIFORM OR COMPANY UNIFORM—UHF radio frequency on which the team or company communicates. Frequencies were changed periodically in an attempt to confuse the enemy.

THREE—Radio call sign of the operations officer.

THREE CORPS—Military area around Saigon. Vietnam was divided into four corps areas.

TO&E—Table of Organization and Equipment. A detailed listing of all the men and equipment assigned to a unit.

TOC—Tactical Operations Center.

TOT—Time Over Target. Refers to the time the aircraft is supposed to be over the drop zone with parachutists, or the target if the plane is a bomber.

TRICK CHIEF—NCOIC for a shift.

TRIPLE A—Antiaircraft Artillery or AAA. Anything used to shoot at airplanes and helicopters.

TWO—Radio call sign of the intelligence officer.

TWO-OH-ONE (201) FILE—Military records file that listed all of a soldier's qualifications, training, experience and abilities. It was passed from unit to unit so that the new commander would have some idea about the capabilities of an incoming soldier.

UMZ—Ultramilitarized Zone. The name GIs gave to the DMZ (Demilitarized Zone).

UNIFORM—Refers to the UHF radio. Company Uniform would be the frequency assigned to that company.

USARV—United States Army, Vietnam.

VC—Vietcong, called Victor Charlie (phonetic alphabet) or just Charlie.

VIETCONG—Contraction of Vietnam Cong San (Vietnamese Communist).

WHITE MICE—Referred to the South Vietnamese military police who wore white helmets.

WIA—Wounded In Action.

WILLIE PETE—WP, white phosphorus, called smoke rounds. Also used as antipersonnel weapons.

WOBBLY ONE—Refers to a W-1, the lowest warrant officer grade. Helicopter pilots who weren't commissioned started out as Wobbly Ones.

WORLD—The United States.

WSO—Weapons Systems Officer. The name given to the man who rode in the back seat of a Phantom because he was responsible for the weapons systems.

XM-21—Name given to the Army's sniper rifle, an M-14 mounted with a special ART scope.

XO—Executive officer of a unit.

X RAY—Refers to an engineer assigned to a unit.

ZAP—To ding, pop caps or shoot. To kill.

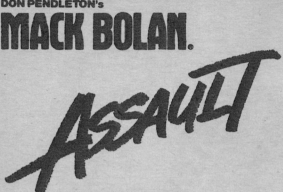